THE OTHER HANDBOOK

THE OTHER HANDBOOK

Credits

Creator/Lead Design: Bryan Donihue (One-Legged GM)

Development Team: Bryan Donihue, Michael "Imp" Tipton, Danielle "WD-42" Thomas, Simon "Ghost" Verburg, Jessie "Grace" Stevenson, David "Spooky" Cassiday,

Editors: Laura "L-Wray" Hewitt, David "Spooky" Cassiday

Graphic Design and Layout: Bryan Donihue

Artists: Rob "The Badger" O'Neil, Bryan Donihue, Christy McCulfor

Cover Design: Rob "The Badger" O'Neil

Stock Photography: Adobe Stock, Depositphotos

Playtesters: *Thank you to this amazing list of playtesters responsible for breaking this game. You folks make it better.*

Simon "Ghost" Verburg, Jessie "Grace" Stevenson, Paul "Glitch" Greenwald, Michael "Imp" Tipton, Danielle "WD-42" Thomas, Spenser "Vlad" Nordstrom, Theran "Neuro" Nordstrom

Bryan Donihue | One-Legged GM

Grand Rapids, Michigan

Website: www.incursionlegends.com

YouTube: youtube.com/one-leggedgm

Discord: bit.ly/s28discord

Facebook: facebook.com/incursionlegends

Signature Panel

DEVELOPMENT TEAM

EDITORS / PROOFREADERS

PLAYTESTERS

ARTISTS

CONTENTS

Forward

It may seem unusual for a paranormal game book, but this book is first and foremost dedicated to Jesus, the Christ - the only true Savior who can save us from evil. He is the real source of Hope.

This game is dedicated to my wife, Christina, and my brood of kids. You've put up with many months of my unavailability while I was writing and many weekends where I am traveling to comic cons. Thank you for putting up with me and my obsession with telling stories.

I had a couple wonderful editors on this project, Laura Hewitt and David Cassiday. They worked diligently to make sure that I explained the rules clearly and correctly, used correct grammar and style, and made sure that this game is the best that we can create. They made sure that I didn't screw up all the little details, while also making sure that the rules made sense. They are also great friends who are not afraid to tell me when I screw things up. In that, they are awesome editors.

Any and all of the mistakes that are left in this book are solely mine, usually because I didn't listen to Laura and David.

This book came about because our fans wanted to play the monsters. As we were developing Hidden Worlds Refined Core, I figured it was the perfect time to launch this project. Who were the guinea pigs? My gamers on my One-Legged GM YouTube channel. They helped develop the concept behind the playable Others. The playtest development group is:

- Simon "Ghost" Verburg
- Jessie "Grace" Stevenson
- Danielle "WD-42" Thomas
- Michael "Imp" Tipton
- Paul "Glitch" Greenwald
- Theran "Neuro" Nordstrom
- Spenser "Vlad" Nordstrom

I hope you enjoy playing an Other as much as we've enjoyed creating this book.

> **The setting for this game is based on an original world created by Bryan Donihue. The game mechanics originated in an original roleplaying game created by Troye Gerard, Bryan Donihue, and David Cassiday. The "Section 28" name idea was originally from Troye, and he graciously allowed me to twist it to my own particular flavor.**

OFFICE OF TRANSHUMAN AFFAIRS
VIGILANTI CONTRA NOX
SECTION 28

Special Agent Brianna Wilcox crouched at the edge of the doorway. She closed her eyes to concentrate, listening for the sounds from the next room. The relatively new vampire heard furtive movements, and then she heard the quiet, metallic "snick" through the thin interior walls. She recognized the sound from her pre-vampire days–someone had disengaged a firearm safety. She turned and flashed a sign to the member of the entry team behind her. "Weapons inside," the signal flashed. The entry team member behind her repeated the sign down the line.

The team was stacked for entry outside of a suspected dealer's apartment. This was not a typical drug dealer. There was a brand new drug hitting the streets, and it was becoming the most popular, and deadly drug in the area. The Office of Transhuman Affairs was there to shut down the dealer and their production center before the drug went nationwide. Agent Wilcox was leading the team that was charged with bringing down the dealer. Once they took down the dealer and her lieutenants, they would interrogate the survivors and find and shut down the production center. Hard.

Knowing that she was the lead entry, Agent Wilcox nervously rubbed her tongue along the inside of her razor-sharp teeth. Still not used to the impossibly sharp molars, she unconsciously rubbed across them every time she changed. She felt a double tap on her shoulder. The team lead signaled that everyone was ready. The vampire government agent took a deep breath and prepared to spring forward.

Wilcox exploded forward in a burst of speed and energy, her vampire abilities enhancing her natural strengths and abilities. She kicked in the door, noticing that it slammed into the wall and stuck fast, the doorknob buried in the plaster. The vampire dove through the doorway, rolling on her shoulder and coming up, her suppressed MP-5N submachine gun raised and tracking the first movement she saw. She stroked the trigger twice, sending a three-round burst of slugs into the target each time.

The first burst took the startled terrorist in the chest. As she pulled the trigger a second time, time seemed to slow as her vampiric senses kicked in. She watched as the second trio of silver-laced hollowpoints slammed into the face of the target, and she recognized the canine face and elongated muzzle of a werewolf. The muzzle disintegrated as the rounds slammed through it and into the skull of the beast.

The other three members of the entry team filed through the door at a fast walk, peeling off in different directions to cover the interior. Wilcox heard movement to her left and whirled to confront the new threat. She was not fast enough. She felt the bullet hit her side, find its way through the slight gap between her armor and her armpit, and slam into her ribs. The pain was intense and immediate.

Pushing past the agony, she continued her turn, falling backward to get out of the way of the other bullets hurtling her way. Landing on her back caused her wound to flare with intense agony. Through the pain, the agent saw her attacker fumbling with his pistol. He dropped the now-empty magazine and reached for a fresh one. Before he could reload his gun, she raised the barrel of her own and again stroked the trigger twice. Six more rounds erupted from the end of the agent's sub gun. All six rounds hit her target, shredding the chest of the man. As the man fell, Wilcox took her attention from the dead man and looked around the room.

She heard shouts and gunshots from other areas of the apartment. Wilcox rose and climbed to her feet, wincing as she reopened the wound under her arm. The vampire agent groaned, knowing that she would have to have surgery to dig out the bullet that was lodged in her chest. She was suddenly hungry as her body pulled from its own reserves to heal the internal damage caused by the bullet stuck in her chest.

Agent Wilcox raised her submachine gun to her shoulder, holding it angled down in the traditional low-ready position. One more look around the living room she was standing in, and then she started moving forward, heading toward the rear of the apartment. A few moments later, she rendezvoused with the rest of the entry team and they stopped to take stock of the situation.

Four of the apartment's occupants had been shot and killed in the entry. They were able to take the dealer into custody. She was currently facedown on the floor with her hands tied behind her with zip ties. Wilcox indicated to the drug dealer on the floor, "Let's pick her up and sit her in a chair. We're on the clock on this one."

Two of her team members grabbed the drug dealer, one under each arm. They lifted the dealer up to her feet and dropped her unceremoniously in a nearby chair. Wilcox watched the prisoner as she was dumped into the chair. The dealer glared at the team, baring her teeth at the agent on her left arm and growling.

"Where's your lab, Nora?" Wilcox knelt down and looked her in the eye. "Where are you producing the Dragon's Eye?"

Dragon's Eye was the street name of the new designer drug that activated certain higher-conscious functionality in the user's mind. The sample obtained by the OTA tested as almost pure oxycodone cut with faerie pixie dust. Some pixies were being harvested, and both the Seelie Court and the Office of Transhuman Affairs were desperate to take down the operation. Nora Wildewood was a local dryad, a faerie born of and linked to a specific tree. While dryad were normally tied to the Seelie Court, Nora was a wild dryad and had aligned herself with the Unseelie King. She was building her empire.

Nora glared at Special Agent Wilcox. She growled under her breath, "I wouldn't tell you anything. You should be ruling these… humans. Instead, you have chosen to be a slave to the inferior race."

Wilcox smirked, letting the tips of her fangs show. She kept her voice low and steady, sarcasm dripping from her words, "I am the one that is free right now, my little wood nymph. I'm going to give you one opportunity to tell us where your production facilities are."

The dryad cursed, turning the air blue with invectives. Agent Wilcox nodded and leaned even closer. She whispered into Nora's ear, "You will break." She leaned back and keyed her radio. "Gummer, this is Boots. I need a demonstration."

Three blocks away, another team was staked out in a local park. They had approached and sought out a very special tree. Dryads typically stayed as close to their tree as possible, and the Seelie Court had tracked Nora's tree down to this park. Once they identified Nora's tree, the four-person team had staked it out in anticipation of this radio call.

Michael "Gummer" Wilcox was a tall, lanky agent with a mustache that made him look like the iconic gun-loving survivalist played by Michael Gross. His call sign was an obvious choice. Gummer was married to the agent currently interrogating the drug-dealing dryad named Nora. Looking around for any human or fae guardians, he keyed his radio, "Boots, Gummer. Copy on a small demonstration."

The tall agent grinned at the other agents, revealing the sharpened teeth of a vampire. As he leaned down and picked up an ax, Gummer nodded at the other agents. "Watch my back. Once I hit the tree, any guardian fae will be hitting us in force." The three other agents nodded and turned outward, watching for attackers. Michael grabbed the ax handle with both hands and drew it back to strike. The silver edge of the blade contrasted with the cold-forged iron of the head itself. Calling on the strength of his own monster, the tall agent swung the twelve-pound ax head and slammed it into the trunk of the tree.

The park around them shook as if an earthquake had rolled through. The OTA Action Team struggled to stay on their feet. A scream from the forest around them alerted the agents as another dryad exploded out of the tree line. The agent to Gummer's left opened up with her suppressed submachine gun. The dryad twisted out of the way, and the silver-coated rounds ripped into the forest beyond. The wild dryad slammed her arm into the agent who shot at her, sending the OTA agent flying away from Nora's tree.

The dryad slammed her shoulder into Gummer and crashed to a stop. The vampire laughed, "My turn." Using a tight one-handed grip high on the ax handle, he swung from his waist and buried the silver-tipped iron head into the chest of the dryad. Her howls of rage quickly changed to screams of pain as the silver and iron interacted with her faerie blood. Moments later even her screams faded away as she slumped over the ax head.

Gummer shook the now-dead fae from the end of the ax head and keyed his radio, "Boots, this is Gummer. What's your status?"

Three blocks away, the other Agent Wilcox could barely hear her husband over Nora's shrieks of agony. Reaching out, "Boots" Wilcox grabbed the hair on Nora's head and

lifted the thrashing dryad's face to her own. "What do you say, little wood nymph? Do I have your attention, yet?"

The dryad moaned in pain, and Wilcox saw blood running down the right leg of the dryad. Her husband's cut into the tree had injured the nymph physically. Kicking the injured leg right on the wound, Wilcox hissed, "C'mon, Nora. I don't have any patience. The next time I contact my agent, he's going to take your tree down. Permanently."

The tree nymph's eyes widened in panic. She was stuttering as she responded, "No. Don't take my tree. I'll tell you what you want. It's outside town, in Hunter's Woods. There's an old fire access road that leads to an abandoned warehouse. It's off Route 23."

Keying her radio, she called out, "Did you get all that, Spooky?"

She heard his reply in her earpiece, "Copy that, Boots. Tasking a drone now. Wait one."

Wilcox waited, letting go of the sobbing dryad's hair. She glanced down at the plastic cuffs restraining the prisoner. They were glowing a brighter glow in the black and white vision of her monster, and a faint line of Enochian was visible, showing that the specially enchanted cuffs were keeping the fae restrained.

The vampire agent heard Spooky's voice in her ear, "Got it, Boots. I've got eyes on the target and I see a lot of activity around there. Thermal shows twenty-two people, most of them human or fae. No signs of the pixies. Cameras can confirm large amounts of a white powder substance and an assembly line. Same type of packaging as the Dragon's Eye we found earlier."

Wilcox raised Nora's face again, "Where are the pixies?"

Nora sobbed, "Dead. Sent out a team to capture more. They never returned."

Wilcox showed a cruel grin, "That's because I got to 'em first." She released Nora's head again, and talked to Spooky, "You got that? Do you show any pixie-sized readings?"

"Negative, no pixies on the thermal or UVR."

"Send it to my phone." Wilcox pulled her secure phone from one of the pouches on her vest. Almost immediately, she received a video feed from Spooky's drone. "Is there anyone else within a mile of that location, Spooky?"

"No, ma'am. Nothing on any of the drones."

"Perfect. Send in the strike. Attack load Peregrine. Level the area."

"Strike package Peregrine will be inbound to target in thirty-five minutes." The electronics specialist chuckled to himself, "Spooky, calling in the Spooky."

Thirty-four minutes later, the drone of four turboprop engines from the darkened AC-130U "Spooky" aircraft was heard as it approached the target area. Inside the plane, the pilot called over the radio, "Nightrider One approaching target area now. Confirm weapons free."

The special aircraft controller assigned to the gunship looked at the Air Force colonel standing over their shoulder. The colonel nodded and the controller passed it on. "Affirmative Nightrider One. Confirm weapons free. Target package is confirmed."

Aboard the gunship, the pilot acknowledged, then keyed his intercom. "Attention gunners. Confirmed target package. Fire when ready."

Almost immediately, the plane shuddered as the 105mm artillery cannon opened up. Four minutes later, the last of the 25mm incendiary rounds lanced into the ruins of the warehouse and outbuildings. Four of the 105mm artillery rounds had started the destruction, and those had been followed by several rounds of the 40mm shells, followed up by a couple of short bursts from the 25mm Gatling gun to clean up the attack.

As the gunship circled the flattened ruins, the pilot called back to the air controller. "Nightrider One to Control. Target is destroyed. Returning to base."

"Affirmative, Nightrider One. Vector one-one-zero, cleared to flight level two-two. Traffic cleared all the way back to base. Contact approach on Channel Six."

Back in the apartment, Agent Wilcox listened to Spooky's report in her ear. She acknowledged the report and looked down with pity at the broken dryad before her. "Your warehouse and distribution are gone, Nora. We're going to take you before the Seelie Queen. I understand she has some rather pointed questions about her missing pixies."

Nora Wildewood, the battered and broken dryad, whimpered as she considered what the Queen would do to her. Rather, what the Queen's Pixie Maidens would do to her.

Welcome to the Other Handbook

The game, *Hidden Worlds*, is designed to be played as a human character. After we released the game, one of the first requests was to release a supplement that supported non-human, or partially human, player characters. This book is the result.

What is in *The Other Handbook?*

The Created Others: This section details the alternate character creation options that can replace creating a fully human character. This includes Dhampir, Faelings, Demigods, Cryptids, and even Mad Scientist Constructs. This section will REPLACE standard character creation for those player characters.

The Changed Others: This section details alternate character options that take place at the end of character creation, or even during the game. The player character starts as a fully human character, and the created other MODIFIES the standard character. This includes Vampires, Therianthropes, and even Corrupted cult members.

The Gamemaster: This section discusses using the Others as player characters in the campaign. This includes balancing Other and non-Other characters, Running an Others-only campaign, and some additional Story Hooks for your campaigns.

The World of the Other: This section discusses some of the cultures surrounding some of the more common Other Player Characters. This section also explores how those often-hidden subcultures interact with the "normal" world around them.

This is **NOT** a Standalone Book!

This is a supplement specifically written for Hidden Worlds: Incursion. You will need access to the game manual in some form. If you do not have that available, it can be found on our website: https://www.incursionlegends.com/store

You will also need the Other Character Sheet for HW: I. If you do not have one, you can download them directly from our website: https://www.incursionlegends.com/downloads

You will need a single d20 (physical or electronic).

You will need some sort of marking utensil, a pencil is recommended.

And you will need a GM who will put up with the antics of you and your fellow gamers. If you ARE the GM? My sympathies. I'm kidding–mostly. We have put a section in the back of this book specifically for you. That section will include tips for balancing the encounters, creating encounters, and even tips to handle the munchkin demigod players in your game.

Potential Ickiness Ahead

This is a good point to remind you, the reader, that the origin story of most monsters, what we call Others, can be problematic for themes that might be addressed in the Safety Tools we mentioned in the *Hidden Worlds Refined Core.* Vampire and werewolf infections are almost always non-voluntary infections. The gods of the Greek and Roman pantheons often used questionable methods, including deception, to have progeny with humans, and the fae are notorious for deception and the theft of children. And, in our case, the experimental victims of mad scientists can be held and experimented on without their consent, a la those unfortunate victims of Dr. Moreau.

We want to strongly recommend players and GMs consider the people in the group when they are creating Other characters. If you are using the recommended Safety Tools, make sure the character's backstories are not crossing any lines or subjects that are off limits.

Speaking of limits…

Because of Zeus, We Can't Have Nice Things…

No, Nate, you can't be a vampire-demigod-gerbilthrope. Why? Because a blood-sucking furball with the power of the gods is even more terrifying than your sasquatch-chihuahuathrope. That's why.

PLAYABLE RACES
CHAPTER ONE

THE PLAYABLE OTHERS

In the Hidden Worlds, any sapient, non-human beings that inhabit the world are considered "Others". From the sasquatch and the other naturally occurring cryptids to the ethereal fae, and from the mythological monsters straight out of horror movies to the gods worshipped in the various pantheons around the world, the Others live amongst humanity, whether they realize it or not. The history of humans and non-humans is interwoven in this realm, and the Others have been in hiding for most of it. Until the Dragonfire Incident, secret forces in the various governments kept all incidents and records of the existence of Others relegated to the bins of innuendo and conspiracy theories. Then the world became aware that other, non-human beings walked among the populace.

In the game, *Hidden Worlds*, the players play human characters that are charged with either keeping the secrets (before the Dragonfire Incident) or keeping the peace (after Dragonfire). In this manual, we are introducing specific playable Others as alternate races for the player characters. Why is this selection limited? Balance. The goal is to make any playable races balanced enough to be unique and fun, without absolutely breaking the game or overshadowing every other character in the game. Want an example? It is far easier to balance a vampire character versus an elder god. If Cthulhu climbs out of the agency van, it does not matter who the other characters are representing. No one wants to play a human if Cthulhu is available, right?

This is also the reason that full gods and full fae are not playable races. They are generally too powerful to be balanced as player characters. Their half-breed offspring? Those are fair game. To this end, we have divided the playable Others into two basic types: Created Others and Changed Others.

Created Others are those that are Others from birth, or creation. Demihumans like demigods, half-fae, and dhampir all share a half-human heritage. Also in the Created Others are the humanoid cryptids like sasquatch and lizardfolk. Rounding out Created Others are golem-like constructs made of flesh, metal, or rock.

Changed Others all started out as humans. Vampires and their emotion-feeding vampyre cousins suffer from a mutated fae-based curse and are included in the Changed Others. Therianthropes such as werewolves are the shape-shifting Others who suffer from a similar fae-based curse as Changed Others. The Changed Others also include the poor souls who have been so afflicted with eldritch energy that they are corrupted on a path to redemption. Rounding out the Changed Others are the genetic or chemical experimental subjects of mad scientists.

WHERE DO THE CHARACTERS FIT?

Where do the Others fit in the world as player characters? Anywhere human characters fit, usually. If the campaign is post-Dragonfire, the characters can either be a part of the Office of Transhuman Affairs (OTA) or part of an independent agency as any other human character. Pre-Dragonfire, the Other characters will have to be even more circumspect than human agents hunting monsters, but it is still a very playable era.

THE CREATED OTHERS

The Created Others are those beings that have never been fully human. They were born or created as the Other they are. As far as playable Others, the created Others are separated into three different primary categories: Demihumans, Cryptids, and Constructs.

DEMIHUMANS

As the Created Others that are closest to human, demihumans are born of mixed parentage of a human parent and an Other parent. Even if they are accepted by their Other parent, demihumans are generally not accepted by the society and culture of their Other heritage. Although they usually have a better chance of fitting in with human society, demihumans often have a mixed track record with their human parent, based on the circumstances of their creation. As a result of their cross-breeding, demihumans are naturally sterile. There are four playable races of demihumans in the *Hidden Worlds*: Dhampir, Dhamphyr, Demigod, and Faeling.

DHAMPIR

When a vampire bites and infects a pregnant human woman who is near to full term on her pregnancy, the woman passes her infection on to her child. Due to the trauma and infection of the virus, the woman almost immediately enters labor. If the child survives the traumatic birth, they are a new vampire/human hybrid unleashed on the earth. The new dhampir's mother either continues turning into a vampire due to the original infection or dies during the trauma of infection during childbirth.

Dhampir have some of the strengths of their vampire heritage, however, they have few of the vampire vulnerabilities. Sunlight and UV light do not affect the dhampir, they are free to walk about during the day without harm. Unlike their vampire heritage, silver does not damage dhampir when it touches them, however, silver will inhibit the dhampir's healing abilities.

While the dhampir does not need or crave blood normally, they can use fresh blood to rejuvenate and jumpstart their faster-than-normal healing. Unfortunately, overindulging in blood as a stimulant and healing factor can lead to a craving or addiction for fresh blood.

The dhampir generally has no standing in a vampire coven or society. They are looked upon as mongrels or servants at best. Some dhampir choose to act as coven guards or daytime business managers to ingratiate themselves into vampire society. Others choose to side with their human cousins and work for hunter teams, using their vampire strengths to seek out and terminate the very monsters that made them.

DHAMPHYR

Like their dhampir cousins, dhamphyr are the product of a vampyre infecting a near-term pregnant woman. Like the dhampir, the woman with the vampyre infection passes it along to her unborn child. The infection immediately induces labor, and if the child survives, it is born as a new dhamphyr. The child's mother either will continue her transformation into a vampyre due to the original infection or dies due to the combined trauma of childbirth and infection.

Dhamphyr only retain some of the strengths and capabilities of their vampyre heritage, however, they are not plagued by as many of their vulnerabilities. Dhamphyr are not susceptible to the same sunlight and UV restrictions of their vampyre heritage, leaving them free to walk about in broad daylight. Although silver will inhibit the healing of a dhamphyr, its touch will not harm them directly.

The dhamphyr can accelerate their internal spiritual healing by feeding off of the emotions surrounding them, however, they do not require emotional turmoil to survive. Unfortunately for the dhamphyr, frequent direct spiritual feeding may lead them to crave or become addicted to the energy and process of feeding.

Dhamphyr are even less welcome among the vampyre covens than their dhampir cousins. Because of the seductive nature of the vampyre, it is far easier for the covens to have followers do the grunt work and act as guards during the daylight hours. Most dhamphyr try to remain unnoticed by both the human and vampyre worlds, with few deciding to actively hunt the Others in their heritage.

DEMIGOD

When a deity spends time on earth and decides to mate with a mortal human, their offspring is a mortal with some of the deity's characteristics, and some of their flaws. While the mother is normally the mortal party, there is precedence where the deity has been female and gets impregnated by a mortal male. Either way, pregnancy, and gestation are usually pretty typical for a human being.

Demigods are mortal, and age as a mortal ages. Their shared heritage with the deity also means that demigods gain some of their Other parent's power and capabilities. Unfortunately, demigods also inherit some of their deity parent's deific flaws as well.

While demigods are not normally accepted by their deity parent's pantheon, they are usually human enough to be accepted by human society at large, at least until their demigod quirks surface. In truth, a lot of demigods find a way to become a part of human society, finding their niche. It is only those that have the far more dangerous quirks of their deific heritage that become pariahs of their human heritage as well.

All the arroogance of a god,
none of the immortality!
— G'snoort

Faeling

The offspring of a fae parent and a human parent is called many terms, with faeling being the most commonly used. The demifae inherits some of the benefits of their fae heritage, while also gaining some of the flaws and weaknesses of the fae. Faelings are mortal due to their heritage, and their lifespan reflects their humanity.

Because of their fae heritage, they are susceptible to several of the fae's weaknesses, including pure silver and cold iron. Their words have power, and bargains struck are bargains kept with faelings, much like their fae progenitors. As a faeling, they also can draw some power from their thin connection to the fae, based on their specific heritage.

Faelings are generally despised by those from the fae realm. Full-blooded fae look at faelings as mongrels, devoid of value, and having been soiled irreparably by the taint of their human blood. Even those fae that are a cross between two different types of fae look down upon the faelings. In fae society, faelings are referred to with the derogatory "mallacta," which means "cursed." If there are multiple faelings, or discussing faelings in general, those from Álfheimer will often use "mallactaí", or the cursed ones.

Faelings have a better time fitting into human society, as their fae nature allows them to have a minor glamour, fitting in with those around them. This often means subtle changes to any non-human appearance, including skin color, ear shape, or hair. Depending on the circumstances, the faelings often stand a better chance of bonding with their human parent than their fae parent, and most faelings are relegated to surviving in human society without a deep connection to fae society.

Sapling's coffee is the best. Boomer says it's gremlin meth, without the bad teeth.
— G'Snoort

CRYPTIDS

Cryptids are those creatures natural to the earth's realm, but who have survived throughout history as part of legend or myth, staying away from humanity as much as possible. This distance was often the best survival method for cryptids, allowing them to develop and thrive without being hunted to extinction. Because they have survived for centuries out of the spotlight of human society, cryptids generally have a deep aversion to being a part of human society, with very few exceptions. There are four types of cryptids that are playable Others in *Hidden Worlds*: Simians, Reptilians, Winged, and Canids.

SIMIANS

The simian cryptids are those that are typically the most ape-like, or human-like in existence. The most common simian-type cryptids are the Sasquatch and the Yeti, although the Skunk Ape and Swamp Thing are also simian cryptids. Both the sasquatch and yeti are figures out of myth and legend. Sasquatch are often seen in the woods and forests in North America, while the yeti are most often seen or rumored to be in the mountains of Europe and Asia.

While there have been many purported sasquatch sightings in North America, the vast majority of them have been wrong enough to mischaracterize the size and characteristics of the typical sasquatch. Although they do have large feet, unlike the legends, sasquatch tend to be average human height, if not shorter. In fact, one of the most infamous sasquatch on the net is under five feet tall. The average sasquatch is very muscular to the point of stocky and tends to have long, coarse hair that is usually black or dark brown, although they turn gray and white as they age and get near their end of life. Sasquatch tend to live in large extended clan-like families, often comprised of several generations of the cryptids surviving together, and sasquatch elders are generally the leaders of the families.

Unlike their social cousins, the yeti are famously loners and choose to live solitary lives, coming together only to mate. Yeti are fiercely territorial, and the constant struggle for territory has kept their population very low. Almost the opposite of sasquatch, yeti tend to be very tall, upwards of seven or eight feet tall, thin, and covered in a short, thick coarse white, or light blond/tan fur.

Skunk Apes are very similar to sasquatch, coming from the same original creatures. They are often found in the southeast forests and swamps. Skunk apes are almost as solitary as the yeti, although they are not nearly as territorial with other skunk apes. Another simian cryptid living in the swamps of the southeastern United States is the swamp thing. Not much is known of these cryptids, although they tend to be very rare and solitary. They get their name from their habit of moving through the swamps enough to gather a natural camouflage of vegetation, mud, and seaweed that becomes matted in their thick, coarse hair.

Do NOT call any sasquatch "Bigfoot." Apparently, no one likes him. — G'Snoort

REPTILIANS

Also known as lizardmen, the reptilian cryptids are adept at blending in with human society. Their long lives and innate glamour abilities to look like humans allow a class of them to build family dynasties of both wealth and political power. Reptilians are not aliens, they are a natural race that evolved on earth, and some anthropological experts have theorized that the lizard-folk are some of the reasons for the "uncanny valley" aversion in humans.

When not using their glamour, reptilians are hairless, have scaly skin, and moderately humanoid features. Bipedal, they are often about average human height and tend to be thin and muscular. The reptilian glamour is innate and is automatically created when they are around people. Most reptilians can vaguely sense when a non-human is using glamour around them, however, the proliferation of Others after the Dragonfire Incident means that they cannot often tell if the person using the glamour is a fellow reptilian, a fae, or a different kind of Other.

Reptilian society is rigidly structured, even within the greater looseness of human society. The elite reptilians are those who have developed the political and economic power to manipulate the human and reptilian worlds. Their natural skin and scales tend toward lighter shades of green. Elites hold power over any of the lesser caste, the drones. Drones tend to have skin with more blues in their scale coloring. Drones also have a single or double dark stripe running from their forehead up and over their scalp, running down their back. If a drone is born without the stripe, they are adopted into and raised as an elite.

WINGED

The winged cryptids are those that generally haunt the night of myth and legend and are fiercely protective of their territory. Mothman sightings, owlman appearances, and gargoyles are three of the most prolific winged humanoid cryptids. Even though they possess large wings, they cannot truly fly. Instead, winged cryptids can glide if dropping from a sufficient height – they "fall with style."

Even without their wings, the winged cryptids would generally be unable to physically blend into human society. Moth-folk and bird-folk cryptids often have features that live up to their nicknames. Even though both kinds of cryptids are humanoid, moth-folk tend to have insect-like features including ears that are extended and almost look like antennae, with large moth-like wings. Their mouth and nose tend to be a bit thinner and drawn. Bird-folk like the owlman have more avian features, with fine, down-like hair and a sharper nose and feathered, bird-like wings with claws instead of regular arms. Moth-folk and bird-folk tend to be solitary cryptids, although the mother of offspring will stay with their offspring until they are old enough to be on their own.

Gargoyles are different entirely. Gargoyle skin is rough and mottled gray, reflecting the texture of stone, without the rigidity and protection of stone. With the sharp, chiseled features of a statue, gargoyles are traditionally found in the heights of large city centers. The stone statues on church buildings were modeled after the shorter living gargoyles. Gargoyles average about four feet tall with long arms and legs and have bat-like wings on their shoulders.

Unlike the moth-folk and the bird-folk, gargoyles gather in close-knit family units called clans. They often all protect and live on the same building. Gargoyles are fiercely territorial and protective of their home building. Other than the humans who inhabit or "worship" in the building, gargoyles are quick to defend the building from intruders or those Others who might disrupt the building. Because they prefer to remain out of sight from the world, gargoyles are often silent and unknown protectors of their homes and the humans within.

Canid

The dog-like canid cryptids are different from the werewolves and other therianthropes. Unlike the therianthropes, they do not change shape or form. Instead, the canids are dog-like humanoid cryptids that are forced to hide in the shadows, as their features do not allow them to blend into human society at large. The dog-like cryptids include the Michigan dogmen and the rougarou from the swamps in Louisiana.

The dogmen from Michigan tend to be slightly shorter than average humans with short, coarse fur that tends to be dark brown or black. They have large, canine heads with short, stubby snouts and sharp teeth. Due to their unique physical structures, they have a hard time speaking in any human dialect. When they do speak, it is with a rough guttural voice and are often difficult to understand.

The rougarou is a large wolf-like humanoid that inhabits the swamps and forests in Louisiana and the gulf coast. Often mistakenly called loup-garou, this cajun canid averages seven to eight feet tall and has long coarse black fur. Known in legend for killing chickens and other livestock of the Cajuns, most rougarou are born as rougarou, as opposed to the cursed therianthropes called loup-garou. Like other canids, speaking any human language is difficult for rougarou, and any speech they make is thick, guttural, and often difficult to understand.

Unlike therianthropes, canids are not particularly susceptible to silver or wolfsbane, or any of the traditional werewolf specialty weapons. Due to their natural origins, they are also not as durable and quick healing as therianthropes. They live a normal, although somewhat abbreviated lifespan, somewhere in between normal canines and human averages.

CONSTRUCTS

Between the golems of Jewish traditions and the reconstructed flesh monsters of movie fame, constructs are those humanoid creations that are given the spark of life and become autonomous living creatures through their creator. All constructs are brought to life with a spark from the faith of their creator, and none of them can naturally reproduce. There are three types of constructs that are playable Others in the *Hidden Worlds*: Flesh, Clockwork, and Sculpted Constructs.

FLESH

Flesh constructs, often called "Franks" after the seminal science fiction book by Mary Shelley, find their origins in early science fiction and horror, and are often found supporting Hollywood and the entertainment industry. Regardless of how the body parts are attached, once a spark of life is installed in the creature's brain, the body will animate and a new creature is born. The use of a computer or other electronics can facilitate learning and skills in the flesh construct.

Franks are not considered undead, instead, they are considered a new, living creature, with a spark of life and soul. Flesh construct looks are based on their donor parts and can often change body type and shape as they change parts. As long as a flesh construct wears the right clothing, they can often hide their scars and attachment points for their limbs. Most Franks can speak and act independently enough to pass as a somewhat slow human in society.

Their role in the entertainment industry is complicated and intentionally shrouded in lies and innuendo. Franks have often made appearances as horror movie monsters or their stunt actors, and have found a particular home in small, independent films where the budget for stunts and effects was minimal. Because of their ability to repair themselves with any body parts, and their inability to feel pain, flesh constructs were often the perfect option for those low-budget horror flicks.

The flesh construct's major weakness is its brain. Because their source of life, their spark is installed in their brain, if the head or brain is destroyed, the creature will die, and their original life will be unrecoverable. Because of this, most flesh constructs are very protective of their head, and wearing headgear on dangerous assignments is well warranted.

Glitch is funny. Especially when he uses really short arms.
— G'Snoort

CLOCKWORK

Clockwork constructs are mechanical constructs that have been imprinted with the spark of life. Built of wires, gears, and metal, clockwork constructs are often found as menial or specialized labor, and the use of logic boards and circuitry is recommended to give them extra "thinking" power.

The spark of life in a clockwork construct is installed and found in their Harmonic Oscillator, a specialized piece of old technology that is specially crafted to hold their spark. The somewhat delicate Harmonic Oscillator is housed in their head and makes up part of their thinking "brain" and intelligence. For this reason, any damage to the body can be repaired with the right tools and materials, but damage to the head has a good chance of permanently destroying the clockwork construct. Outright destruction of the Harmonic Oscillator will irrevocably destroy the life and soul of the construct.

Due to their unusual appearance, these mechanical constructs find it difficult to be a part of human society normally. Like the flesh constructs, some clockwork constructs have found purpose and life in the entertainment industry. This comes in the form of either a horror monster or untiring specialized labor. Clockwork constructs are intelligent enough to act independently and can speak and communicate if the appropriate hardware is installed in their current body.

SCULPTED

Sculpted constructs originally started out as statues that were eventually brought to life. The most famous of them is the Jewish folklore of golems. In the Jewish tradition, golems were originally formed of clay and given life by sacred writings buried in the clay or written in the clay. Modern sculpted constructs can be made from most inorganic materials, although they must be composed of only one pure material, and any impurities will create physical weaknesses in their body. Clay is still the material of choice for a lot of the sculpted constructs, and because of that, they are often still called golems.

In sculpted constructs, the spark of life is installed in an often-armored container and buried in the golem's head. In modern sculpted constructs. Their intelligence and independence give the sculpted construct the capability of communication, however, even the faith giving them life is barely enough to facilitate verbal communication. Due to their inorganic makeup, any verbal communication is slow and gravely. Golems are unable to pass as normal in any human society.

Because they are composed of inorganic materials, the sculpted constructs will never pass as human in society and are subsequently relegated to the shadows. They make impressive manual laborers and can repair almost any physical damage to their bodies by applying enough of their original materials. If the Spark of Life container is ever destroyed, its spark, and their life, is forfeit.

THE CHANGED OTHERS

The Changed Others are those who were once fully human and have been changed into an Other, often by severe trauma. When considering the Changed Others, the playable races are the life or soul-draining Vamps, the shapeshifting Therianthropes, the Corrupted who have bargained with their soul, and the Experiments by mad scientists.

VAMP

The vamps are a broad category of Other that lives by feeding on the life energy or soul-energy of other beings around them. Vamps live in the shadows, forced by their very nature to live in darkness, unable to feel the warmth of the sun. To become a creature of the night, a human is infected by another vamp with a virus during a feeding. The virus is a hybrid virus with roots in both the nightmare realm of *Coşmar* and the human realm. Because of this, the vamp maintains a small connection to the Romanian-named nightmare realm, giving them the power of the connection to harvest their food, as well as the vulnerabilities of that connection to purity and light. Vamps can only pass on their virus to humans, other creatures cannot meld with the terrifying virus. There are two types of vamps that are playable in the *Hidden Worlds*: Vampire and Vampyre.

VAMPIRE

Vampires are the traditional monsters that feed on the lifeblood of other creatures. Originally born of the virus from the nightmare realm of *Coşmar*, the vampire is an apex predator, with the weapons and capabilities to match. Because their body is connected to the other realm, they also retain some of the weaknesses of purity and light. The vampire requires the flesh and blood of the living to survive. There are three different stages in the life of a vampire that can be playable in the *Hidden Worlds*: Immature, Living, and Undead. There are two more stages in the death cycle of the vampire, but they are not playable as characters: Master and Ancient Master.

Immature vampires are those that have been turned recently, and the virus has not fully subsumed the creature. They teeter on the edge of human and monster. The immature vampire cannot control their monster and will change when triggered. They become susceptible to the UV rays of sunlight, although they will merely turn red and sunburn very quickly. Because the virus has not spread through all their cells, they do not react as violently to sunlight. Merely holding onto silver will cause the immature vampire pain and discomfort, and any damage caused by silver will take much longer to heal. The immature vampire transitions to the Living vampire the first time they feed on blood. Until that moment, it is technically possible to remove the virus by killing the vampire sire - the vampire who turned them.

Living vampires are those who have fed on the life force of a creature and have now embraced their inner monster. Living vampires have some control over their monster and gain an increase in their strength and ferocity, however, they have become more susceptible to both sunlight and silver as weaknesses. Living vampires develop the claws to go with their fangs, and also develop the ability to use their mental powers to gain control of other beings. This compulsion can become permanent, although that is extremely rare for living vampires to gain thralls. If a living vampire sustains enough damage that they nearly die, under the right conditions they will change into an undead vampire.

Undead vampires are the pure monster. Having died in the traditional sense, sunlight and silver are now terrible enemies of these unnatural creatures. When a living vampire transitions, they also gain an impressive boost in strength and ferocity, as well as the mental power to control and dominate other creatures. Undead vampires become harder to permanently kill. They remain, undead vampires, until they have created enough thralls and matured enough to become a master vampire.

VAMPYRE

Where the vampire feeds on the flesh and blood of other creatures, the vampyre feeds on the raw emotions and essence of others. Originally born of the same virus from the nightmare realm of *Coșmar*, the vampyre variant uses glamour and guile to get close to their victims to feed off their victims. While not given the same offensive weapons as the vampire, they do suffer from some of the same weaknesses. Instead of claws and fangs, the vampyre uses their ethereal beauty to find and feed on their victims. While some vampyre are able to feed from the emotions of a crowd, the fastest, and most satisfying feeding is from direct touch.

When a vampyre feeds directly, a special "mouth" appears on the palm of their hands, looking like the sucker on the bottom of an octopus tentacle or a lamprey's mouth. When their prey is distracted by their touch and attention, the mouth on their palms attaches to the victim's skin and draws their essence directly. Like their vampire cousins, there are three life stages for the playable vampyre: Immature, Living, and Undead. There are two non-playable vampyre stages: Master and Ancient Master.

An immature vampyre is only recently turned and has not fed yet. They are still becoming acclimated to the virus, and have not fully succumbed. This is the stage where sunlight and UV light burns but does not kill, and silver hurts, but not fatally so. Like their vampire brethren, the vampyre can technically be freed from their curse if their sire is found and killed under the right circumstances, freeing the person from their monster. The immature vampire's looks will start to change into their eventual ethereal visage.

Once a vampyre feeds directly, the virus has fully integrated, and they become a living vampyre, with much the same results as their vampire cousins. Instead of the vampyre gaining strength and ferocity, their glamour grows, and they become capable of overwhelming their victims with just their aura. Like the vampire, if a vampyre is brought near enough to death under the right circumstances, they become an undead vampyre, where their weapons, and weaknesses, grow exponentially.

THERIANTHROPE

There are many types of shapeshifters in legend and lore, and many of the tales are true at their core. From werewolves and loup-garou to monstrous werebears and angry weregeese, therianthropes are another nightmare from the realm of *Coşmar*. A therianthrope is a human who has been cursed by the virus hybrid, and who has been forced to meld with the essence of a natural creature from the earth realm. The human can and does, shapeshift into the creature they've been cursed with, and they constantly struggle for dominance with their animal.

Because of their connection to Coşmar, therianthropes are vulnerable to the purity of silver as a metal and can be burned/harmed by simply holding the metal. As with most, the purity of the metal determines the reaction to the metal touching the skin. 'Thropes are also controlled by the lunar cycle, and always change when exposed to the direct light of a full moon. Younger therianthropes may also be forced to change on the days leading up to or just after a full moon, but older 'thropes usually can control themselves.

Therianthropes generally go through a life cycle that lasts around twenty years once they are infected. There are four stages in the life cycle of a therianthrope, and each stage has its own characteristics and weaknesses: Immature, Yearling, Mature, and Aging.

Immature therianthropes are those who have been infected with the virus but have not shifted during their first full moon yet. Until that change occurs, they are developing an increasingly bad silver allergy and an enhanced intolerance for wolfsbane. They cannot transmit the virus to any other human, with the exception of the therion half-breeds, and have the slim possibility of shedding their curse by killing the 'thrope that infected them under specific circumstances. Immature therianthropes gain their regeneration ability, allowing them to heal supernaturally quickly. Immature change into yearlings once they survive their first transformation.

Yearlings are those therianthropes in their first year of infection. They have been through at least one change, and the virus has a complete hold over their body. Yearlings gain the ability to change at will (with effort), and can sometimes control their animal side while they are changed. The yearling's regeneration is enhanced and they can quickly heal wounds not caused by silver. When they shift, the yearling's animal is a slightly larger version of the natural version of their animal, well within natural norms. This does mean that a yearling gerbilthrope becomes a tiny gerbil when shifted.

Mature 'thropes are those who have been infected for at least a year, and generally are considered to be mature up until about year thirteen. Mature therianthropes have even more enhanced healing and find it easier to change between their animal and their human when they wish. When a mature therianthrope changes, they tend to have better control over their animal. Mature therianthropes can also complete a partial shift, transforming only part of their human body into their animal. With that, mature 'thropes can control the size of their shifted animal. The size can be anywhere from a slightly larger version of the natural animal up to, or down to, the size of the human.

Around the age of fourteen, therianthropes are considered Aging and begin preparing for their end-of-life. After years of wrestling for control of their animal, they can easily control their beast when shifted, giving them the power of their beast, with the intellect of a human. Partial shifting and the control of their shifted size is also easy for the shifter at this stage. While their healing factors are the best they will ever have, their allergy to silver and wolfsbane is at the worst they will ever be. Silver burns the aging 'thrope on contact with their fur/skin, and wolfsbane is extremely caustic and terrible. Aging therianthropes who die of old age generally live about twenty years from the time of their infection, with no known cases surviving beyond twenty-two years.

The playable Others are restricted to land-based mammals and are divided into two types of 'thropes: Predator and Prey.

PREDATOR

The Predator therianthropes are comprised of a wide range of predator-type mammals. All predator 'thropes rely on their natural weapons of teeth and claws to take down their prey. Most of them are night hunters and thus have superior vision and hearing. Predators are further divided into large predators and small predators. Large predator therianthropes include: Wolves and large dogs, Lions and other big cats, Bears, and Large boars/pigs. Small predator therianthropes include: Hyenas and smaller dogs, Bobcats and smaller cats, Wolverines, Badgers, Mongoose, and Raccoons.

PREY

The Prey therianthrope is comprised of a wide range of prey-type mammals. Prey rely on their natural defenses and camouflage to survive the predators. As with predators, prey 'thropes are divided into large prey and small prey animals. Large prey therianthropes include: Elephants, Bovine, Moose, Horses, Hippos, Rhinos, Deer, and Mountain Goats. Small prey therianthropes include: Rabbits, Gerbils, Rats, Guinea Pigs, Chinchillas, Squirrels, Otters, Pika, and Chihuahuas and other toy dogs.

CORRUPTED

The Corrupted were once humans who connected with beings from a horror-filled eldritch realm called *Rhy'ctharn*. Those humans who create a pact with eldritch powers soon become corrupted with dark energy. Able to draw on the darkness of the eldritch powers, the corrupted serve their eldritch masters to bring horror to the earth. Because they have soaked into the energies from the eldritch realm, their bodies have become twisted by the dark unnatural energies.

The corrupted who break free from their eldritch masters are called the redeemed. The redeemed still retain the unbreakable connection to *Rhy'ctharn* and sometimes tap into that power to fight back the eldritch horrors. When the corrupted tap into the eldritch realm, they risk a little bit of their soul. If they draw too much from *Rhy'ctharn*, they risk allowing the eldritch horrors control over their body and soul. Once the eldritch have control, the corrupted are lost forever in the mind of the horror that now controls their body.

The redeemed are in a constant war with their own eldritch masters, as well as the eldritch corruption of the earth. When the corrupted and redeemed are in their full human form, they are generally able to fit in with human society. The corrupted are often part of a particular cult or group that worships whichever eldritch horror is their master. When the redeemed escape their cult, they either will hide alone and run away from their former life, or they band together with other redeemed to connect with and save other corrupted. The playable corrupted Others come in two of the redeemed types: Animus and Draeden.

ANIMUS

The animus redeemed have been so corrupted and twisted by the dark eldritch energies that they are able to physically change their body into an eldritch warrior form. Their skin morphs into thick, roughened armor, and their arms and fingers elongate into rough cephalopod-like tentacles. With a musculature that twists their form into the shape of an eldritch horror, the animus becomes a frightening warrior.

As with all corrupted, the animus redeemed has the ability to sense other corrupted or eldritch energy around them. When fighting other corrupted, or the eldritch creatures themselves, the redeemed animus is able to summon enough energy to banish another corrupted or eldritch horror, at least until the next nightfall. They are also able to draw their enemy's life essence to heal their own body.

DRAEDEN

Where the animus redeemed draw from the physical characteristics of their former eldritch masters, the draeden are able to harness the horror and other-ness of the eldritch realm and use darkness to terrorize their enemies. Instead of changing into a twisted eldritch physical form, the draeden can make themselves into shadows and shades of darkness, using their mental capabilities to stun their opponents with eldritch terror.

The draeden can sense the eldritch energies around them, like their animus brethren. When they fight eldritch horrors or other corrupted, the draeden can tap into the *Rhy'ctharn* and temporarily banish their enemies back to the eldritch realm. Like the other redeemed, the draeden risks further corruption every time they draw on their eldritch power.

EXPERIMENT

The experiments of mad scientists used to be fully human until the mad scientist got a hold of them. Whether the experiment was kidnapped and experimented on, voluntarily agreed to be a test subject, or was a scientist who experimented on themselves, these beings are no longer fully human. Instead, these new creatures are far beyond normal and are new paranormal Others.

Regardless of the type of experiment, they all have some characteristics in common. The experiments all have the ability to push beyond their normal endurance, reaching deep and drawing on their own essence to heal themselves to survive another day. Due to the nature of their creation, experiments tend to be virtual escape artists, having learned to physically or socially extract themselves from untoward situations.

The experimental Others tend to be survivors of great trauma, and have become fearless in their interactions with humanity. Most of the experimental Others become loners once they find their freedom, and will often fight fiercely before being taken back into custody.

The playable experimental Others are divided into two types: Gene-spliced and Chemical.

GENE-SPLICED

Gene-spliced experiments are those where a scientist has genetically altered a human to be something more, or less than human. The original human DNA has been genetically altered and spliced with the DNA of a natural creature. Those natural creatures can be anything from insects and birds to reptiles and mammals, with only one creature at a time being able to be genetically spliced into a human. Examples of the gene-spliced experiments often found in science fiction, from the human fly to those poor victims of Dr. Moreau.

Gene-spliced experiments all turn out to be bipedal and in a roughly human form. Unfortunately, that is the extent of the humanity that is normally present with these Others. Gene-spliced experiments always display at least some characteristics of their spliced animal, often displaying drastic physical defects as well. While they gain some of the benefits of their spliced code, they also will always end up with weaknesses based on that same spliced code. It is for this reason that gene-spliced experiments often find it incredibly difficult to blend into human society, especially before the Dragonfire Incident.

CHEMICAL

Chemical experiments are those where a scientist has chosen to create a chemical mix to change a human, making them more than human in one specific area of life. The original formula changes and alters the subject incredibly, however, it wears off eventually. Because of the high from the chemical formula, the subject begins to crave the chemical formula. As often happens, the formula soon reaches a point where it has peak effectiveness, but only lasts for a relatively short time. This causes an endorphin swing in the subject and they quickly become addicted to both the chemical formulation and to the endorphin high they reach while on the formula.

These chemicals can be made as a gas, a liquid that must be ingested or absorbed, or a powder that must be ingested for it to work. Once the chemical formulation is reached, the formulation and delivery method does not change. And once a subject has been hooked on the formulation, they can never defeat their addiction to the chemical. Once the subject's body changes to accept the formulation, it will always require at least the minimal amount of that formulation at specified intervals. Depending on how physically deformed the subject gets from the formulation, they may be able to blend into human society, as long as their addiction is kept under control.

DON'T CROSS THE STREAMS

While it may seem possible to combine the effects of one playable Other with another and create a cross-breed, the playable Others are not designed that way. They are currently balanced for play as they sit, and running a dhampir-gerbilthrope hybrid may seem like fun, but the character would be well and truly broken.

If the GM wants to allow such a construct, more power to them, and there are balance topics that will be addressed in the GM chapter. GameMasters: If you are being asked about this or any other non-playable combo, refer to the "What Do I Do With Nate?" section in the GameMaster chapter (page 128).

THE CREATED OTHER

When creating a character that is a Created Other, the basic character creation presented in *Hidden Worlds Refined Core* is modified due to the nature of the Created Others. When building a Created Other, you will substitute standard Attribute calculations and add a new step called "Talents" for your character.

MODIFIED CHARACTER CREATION

STEP 1 - ROLL FOR YOUR ATTRIBUTES

Step one of Character Creation is to roll up your character's Attributes. These form the base of the character's physical, mental, spiritual, and social being. Roll the d20 **nine** different times, and then discard the lowest number. Below you will find eight different attribute charts, one for each Created Other type. Refer to your character's Other type and fill in the attributes with the rolls you just made.

For each attribute chart below, assign a die roll to each Attribute. Each attribute chart has two attributes that can possibly end above (20), and three that are capped below (20). Each Created Other type has a different Attribute chart, except for the Constructs, they all use the same attribute chart.

The Demigods and Faelings also share the same attribute chart, and it is very different from the other attribute charts. For Demigods and Faelings, you will choose which two attributes are the strengths of the character, based on their heritage, and which three attributes are their lowest, again based on their heritage.

ROLL	MIG	HEA	HEC	QCK	ITL	JDG	ALR	LCK
1	8	1	1	5	1	1	1	1
2	8	2	2	5	2	1	1	1
3	8	3	3	5	3	2	2	1
4	9	4	4	6	4	2	2	2
5	9	5	5	6	5	3	3	2
6	10	6	6	7	6	3	3	3
7	11	7	7	8	7	4	4	3
8	12	8	8	9	8	5	4	3
9	13	9	9	10	9	6	5	4
10	15	10	10	12	10	7	5	4
11	16	11	11	13	11	8	6	4
12	17	12	12	14	12	9	6	4
13	18	13	13	15	13	10	7	5
14	19	14	14	16	14	11	7	5
15	20	15	15	17	15	12	8	5
16	20	16	16	17	16	13	9	6
17	21	17	17	18	17	14	10	6
18	22	18	18	19	18	15	11	7
19	23	19	19	20	19	16	12	7
20	25	20	20	22	20	17	13	8

ROLL	MIG	HEA	HEC	QCK	ITL	JDG	ALR	LCK
1	1	5	1	1	1	1	8	1
2	1	5	2	2	2	1	8	1
3	1	5	3	3	3	2	8	2
4	2	6	4	4	4	2	9	2
5	2	6	5	5	5	3	9	3
6	3	7	6	6	6	3	10	3
7	3	8	7	7	7	4	11	4
8	3	9	8	8	8	5	12	4
9	4	10	9	9	9	6	13	5
10	4	12	10	10	10	7	15	5
11	4	13	11	11	11	8	16	6
12	4	14	12	12	12	9	17	6
13	5	15	13	13	13	10	18	7
14	5	16	14	14	14	11	19	7
15	5	17	15	15	15	12	20	8
16	6	17	16	16	16	13	20	9
17	6	18	17	17	17	14	21	10
18	7	19	18	18	18	15	22	11
19	7	20	19	19	19	16	23	12
20	8	22	20	20	20	17	25	13

DEMIGOD AND FAELING

Choose which two attributes are the strengths of the character, based on their heritage, and which three attributes are their lowest, again based on their heritage.

- (Demigod Only) - Choose your character's Pantheon and Divine Heritage (god or goddess).

- (Faeling Only) - Choose your character's Court affiliation and Fae Heritage.

- Pick an attribute to be your character's best attribute based on their heritage then compare the roll of the d20 to the HIGH 1 column

- Pick a second to be your character's next best, again based on their heritage then compare the roll of the d20 to the HIGH 2 column

- Pick an attribute to be your character's weakest, then compare the roll of the d20 to the Low 1 column

- Pick an attribute to be your character's next weakest, then compare the roll of the d20 to the Low 2 column

- Pick an attribute to be your character's least weak, then compare the roll of the d20 to the Low 3 column

ROLL	High (1)	High (2)	Normal	Normal	Normal	Low (3)	Low (2)	Low (1)
1	8	5	1	1	1	1	1	1
2	8	5	2	2	2	1	1	1
3	8	5	3	3	3	2	2	1
4	9	6	4	4	4	2	2	2
5	9	6	5	5	5	3	3	2
6	10	7	6	6	6	3	3	3
7	11	8	7	7	7	4	4	3
8	12	9	8	8	8	5	4	3
9	13	10	9	9	9	6	5	4
10	15	12	10	10	10	7	5	4
11	16	13	11	11	11	8	6	4
12	17	14	12	12	12	9	6	4
13	18	15	13	13	13	10	7	5
14	19	16	14	14	14	11	7	5
15	20	17	15	15	15	12	8	5
16	20	17	16	16	16	13	9	6
17	21	18	17	17	17	14	10	6
18	22	19	18	18	18	15	11	7
19	23	20	19	19	19	16	12	7
20	25	22	20	20	20	17	13	8

ROLL	MIG	HEA	HEC	QCK	ITL	JDG	ALR	LCK
1	8	1	1	1	1	1	1	5
2	8	2	2	1	1	2	1	5
3	8	3	3	2	1	3	2	5
4	9	4	4	2	2	4	2	6
5	9	5	5	3	2	5	3	6
6	10	6	6	3	3	6	3	7
7	11	7	7	4	3	7	4	8
8	12	8	8	4	3	8	5	9
9	13	9	9	5	4	9	6	10
10	15	10	10	5	4	10	7	12
11	16	11	11	6	4	11	8	13
12	17	12	12	6	4	12	9	14
13	18	13	13	7	5	13	10	15
14	19	14	14	7	5	14	11	16
15	20	15	15	8	5	15	12	17
16	20	16	16	9	6	16	13	17
17	21	17	17	10	6	17	14	18
18	22	18	18	11	7	18	15	19
19	23	19	19	12	7	19	16	20
20	25	20	20	13	8	20	17	22

ROLL	MIG	HEA	HEC	QCK	ITL	JDG	ALR	LCK
1	1	1	1	1	8	1	5	1
2	1	1	1	2	8	2	5	2
3	1	2	2	3	8	3	5	3
4	2	2	2	4	9	4	6	4
5	2	3	3	5	9	5	6	5
6	3	3	3	6	10	6	7	6
7	3	4	4	7	11	7	8	7
8	3	5	4	8	12	8	9	8
9	4	6	5	9	13	9	10	9
10	4	7	5	10	15	10	12	10
11	4	8	6	11	16	11	13	11
12	4	9	6	12	17	12	14	12
13	5	10	7	13	18	13	15	13
14	5	11	7	14	19	14	16	14
15	5	12	8	15	20	15	17	15
16	6	13	9	16	20	16	17	16
17	6	14	10	17	21	17	18	17
18	7	15	11	18	22	18	19	18
19	7	16	12	19	23	19	20	19
20	8	17	13	20	25	20	22	20

ROLL	MIG	HEA	HEC	QCK	ITL	JDG	ALR	LCK
1	1	1	5	8	1	1	1	1
2	1	1	5	8	2	2	1	2
3	2	2	5	8	3	3	1	3
4	2	2	6	9	4	4	2	4
5	3	3	6	9	5	5	2	5
6	3	3	7	10	6	6	3	6
7	4	4	8	11	7	7	3	7
8	5	4	9	12	8	8	3	8
9	6	5	10	13	9	9	4	9
10	7	5	12	15	10	10	4	10
11	8	6	13	16	11	11	4	11
12	9	6	14	17	12	12	4	12
13	10	7	15	18	13	13	5	13
14	11	7	16	19	14	14	5	14
15	12	8	17	20	15	15	5	15
16	13	9	17	20	16	16	6	16
17	14	10	18	21	17	17	6	17
18	15	11	19	22	18	18	7	18
19	16	12	20	23	19	19	7	19
20	17	13	22	25	20	20	8	20

ROLL	MIG	HEA	HEC	QCK	ITL	JDG	ALR	LCK
1	1	5	1	1	1	8	1	1
2	2	5	2	2	1	8	1	1
3	3	5	3	3	2	8	2	1
4	4	6	4	4	2	9	2	2
5	5	6	5	5	3	9	3	2
6	6	7	6	6	3	10	3	3
7	7	8	7	7	4	11	4	3
8	8	9	8	8	4	12	5	3
9	9	10	9	9	5	13	6	4
10	10	12	10	10	5	15	7	4
11	11	13	11	11	6	16	8	4
12	12	14	12	12	6	17	9	4
13	13	15	13	13	7	18	10	5
14	14	16	14	14	7	19	11	5
15	15	17	15	15	8	20	12	5
16	16	17	16	16	9	20	13	6
17	17	18	17	17	10	21	14	6
18	18	19	18	18	11	22	15	7
19	19	20	19	19	12	23	16	7
20	20	22	20	20	13	25	17	8

CONSTRUCTS

All three Construct types use this same chart.

ROLL	MIG	HEA	HEC	QCK	ITL	JDG	ALR	LCK
1	5	8	1	1	1	1	1	1
2	5	8	1	2	1	2	1	2
3	5	8	2	3	2	3	1	3
4	6	9	2	4	2	4	2	4
5	6	9	3	5	3	5	2	5
6	7	10	3	6	3	6	3	6
7	8	11	4	7	4	7	3	7
8	9	12	4	8	5	8	3	8
9	10	13	5	9	6	9	4	9
10	12	15	5	10	7	10	4	10
11	13	16	6	11	8	11	4	11
12	14	17	6	12	9	12	4	12
13	15	18	7	13	10	13	5	13
14	16	19	7	14	11	14	5	14
15	17	20	8	15	12	15	5	15
16	17	20	9	16	13	16	6	16
17	18	21	10	17	14	17	6	17
18	19	22	11	18	15	18	7	18
19	20	23	12	19	16	19	7	19
20	22	25	13	20	17	20	8	20

STEP 2 - FILL OUT THE ASPECTS

Step two of Character Creation is where the character's aspects are pulled from the chart below. This is also where the player creates the character's Life Pool and Soul Pool, as well as adding their initial Destiny Pool Point.

ASPECT CHART

First, refer to the chart below. Cross-reference the character's Attributes (MIG, HEC, QCK, and JDG) with the Attribute score for each Aspect.

	MIG		HEC	QCK	JDG
Rank	Throw	Base Strike	Act's	Move	Init
1	2	1(+1)	1	1	1
2	2	1(+1)	1	1	1
3	2	1(+1)	1	1	1
4	3	1(+1)	1	1	2
5	3	1(+1)	1	1	2
6	3	1(+1)	1	1	3
7	3	1(+2)	1	1	3
8	3	1(+2)	2	2	4
9	4	1(+2)	2	2	4
10	4	1(+2)	2	2	5
11	4	1(+2)	2	2	5
12	4	1(+2)	2	2	6
13	4	1(+2)	2	2	6
14	4	1(+3)	2	2	7
15	5	1(+3)	3	2	7
16	5	1(+3)	3	2	8
17	5	1(+3)	3	2	8
18	5	1(+3)	3	2 (+1)	9
19	5	1(+3)	3	2 (+1)	9
20	6	1(+4)	4	3	10
21	6	1(+4)	4	3	11
22	6	1(+4)	4	3 (+1)	12
23	6	1(+5)	4	3 (+1)	13
24	6	1(+5)	4	3 (+1)	14
25	7	1(+6)	5	3 (+2)	15

LIFE POOL

The first step for generating Aspects is to create the character's Life Pool. The character's Life Pool is a measure of their life force. This takes into account injuries received during gameplay and fatigue caused by exhaustion. When this pool drops to zero or below, the character is at risk of dying. To determine your character's Life Pool, add all the Life attributes together. The Life Attributes are Might (MIG), Health (HEA), Hand-Eye Coordination (HEC), and Quickness (QCK). Add all those values together to get the Life Pool.

SOUL POOL

Next, the character's Soul Pool is a measurement of the internal strength and essence of the character. This includes their faith and sanity. When the character uses a Faith Ability, the power is pulled from their Soul Pool. If the character is shocked or suffers from anything that would affect their sanity, that drain will also draw from their Soul Pool. To create the Soul Pool, add together all of the Soul Attributes. They are Intellect (ITL), Judgment (JDG), Allure (ALR), and Luck (LCK). Add those values together to get their Soul Pool.

DESTINY POINTS

The next pool generation is the Destiny Pool. Destiny Points represent the character's importance to fate or destiny. Destiny Points can be used to affect the destiny of the character. If the character is affected by an event, such as an attack or challenge, the character can expend a Destiny Point to change the outcome. The player then describes, in a narrative, how destiny or fate changed the action. The character can also use a Destiny Point to proactively narrate an outcome or story before an event takes place. Every character starts the game with one Destiny Point.

RIGHT-HANDED OR LEFT-HANDED? (OR AMBIDEXTROUS?)

At this stage determine whether your character is either right-handed, left-handed, or ambidextrous (able to use both easily). If your character is going to be ambidextrous, you will need to pick up that Character Trait in the next steps. While it makes no difference here, there are mechanical modifiers for off-hand use of skills, which are found in the *Hidden Worlds Refined Core*, Chapter Three, Playing the Game. Note down which hand is your character's dominant hand.

STEP 3 - ROLL FOR BACKGROUND OR TRAIT

For this step in Character Creation, you will assign at least one Background or Trait to your character. For STEP 3, roll a d20 *ONCE* on the Chart on the next page. The number you rolled provides the background or trait for your character. The text for the background or trait is written below the chart.

Roll	Backgrounds & Traits	Roll	Backgrounds & Traits
1	Orphaned	11	Inheritance
2	Animal Empathy	12	Unlucky
3	Apostate of Faith	13	Sheltered
4	Attractive	14	Graceful
5	Small Obligation to Organization	15	Quick Healer
6	Ugly	16	Impulsive
7	Notoriety	17	Slow Healer
8	Clumsy	18	Apathetic
9	Infamous	19	Fervent
10	Lucky	20	Player's Choice

1. **Orphaned:** The character was an orphan as a child. This character receives a (-5) conditional modifier to any situation that involves trusting institutional leaders. This character also gains a (+3) permanent modifier to the **Survival: Forage** Skill.

2. **Animal Empathy:** The character has a natural affinity for working with and befriending natural animals. This does not apply to "unnatural" or Incursion-based creatures such as dragons or griffons, or Others. Any creature which can be classified as an "other" or a "monster" will not be affected by this ability – GM discretion applies. The character gains a (+3) permanent modifier to **Survival: Taming**.

3. **Apostate of Faith:** This means that your character is an Apostate of their Faith. This means that they no longer believe in their original Faith. This does not mean that they cannot gain Faith or regain their Faith, however, the character receives a (-5) conditional modifier to any Faith-based skill until they restore or gain Faith.

4. **Attractive:** Your character is very good-looking. They gain a (+3) permanent modifier to **Influence: Performance** skill checks.

5. **Small Obligation to Organization:** The character owes a "small" debt or obligation to an organization (legal or illegal). A Small Obligation may require the character to look the other way or to provide certain information at certain times. This debt is not going to come up often, and the "requests" will seem relatively small. This does not usually involve something that will endanger the character directly. This type of debt usually arises from serving with or for the organization for such a length of service that the character feels a loyalty or duty to the organization/person. The character receives (+1) fairly **low-level contact** in that organization.

6. **Ugly:** Your character is ugly to look at. They receive a (-3) permanent modifier to **Influence: Performance** skill checks.

7. **Notoriety:** The character has some notoriety, and their name is known throughout the region for a specific reason. The character gains a (+3)

permanent modifier to the **Influence: Performance** skill and they receive a (-4) conditional modifier to any **Survival: Stealth** attempts to hide, or blend in with the crowd. *NOTE: The player makes suggestions for the reason and scope of the character's "notoriety". The GM has final approval.*

8. **Clumsy:** The character is clumsy. They receive a (-2) conditional modifier to HEC-based Attribute SCs and OCs. *NOTE: This does not include HEC-based skill checks, only Attribute checks.*

9. **Infamous:** This character is infamous and has a bad reputation that is known throughout the region. The character gains a (+3) conditional modifier for **Influence: Negotiation** with criminal elements, and they receive a (-4) conditional modifier for the **Influence** skill during interactions with any law enforcement or military.

10. **Lucky:** This character is very lucky. This character gains a (+4) permanent modifier to the character's **LCK** attribute.

11. **Inheritance:** This character has a sizable inheritance. This could be a collection of vehicles or an estate/house or family business that was passed to the character through their ancestors. This valuable inheritance does come with responsibilities that could include upkeep, taxes, or the like. This character gains **Wealth** (+2).

12. **Unlucky:** The character is just unlucky. The character receives a (-2) permanent modifier to the character's **LCK** attribute.

13. **Sheltered:** This character was sheltered during their early years. This character receives a (-3) permanent modifier to the **Influence** skill.

14. **Graceful:** The character is graceful. They gain a (+2) conditional modifier to HEC-based Attribute SCs and OCs. *NOTE: This does not include HEC-based skill checks, only Attribute checks.*

15. **Quick Healer:** This Trait allows your character to heal their Life Pool at a much more rapid rate. They gain a (+5) conditional modifier to any Life Pool healing SC Attempt. *NOTE: Applies to the Healing Attempt, NOT to the Healing Results.*

16. **Impulsive:** The character is very impulsive, and does not exercise good judgment. The character receives a (-1) permanent modifier to the **JDG** attribute.

17. **Slow Healer:** Your character takes an incredibly long time to heal their Life Pool. The character receives a (-5) conditional modifier to any Life Pool healing SC Attempt. *NOTE: Applies to Healing Attempt, NOT to the Healing Results.*

18. **Apathetic:** Your character takes an incredibly long time to heal their Soul Pool. The character receives a (-5) conditional modifier to any Soul Pool healing SC Attempt. *NOTE: Applies to Healing Attempt, NOT to the Healing Results.*

19. **Fervent:** This Trait allows your character to heal their Soul Pool at a much more rapid rate. They gain a (+5) conditional modifier to any Soul Pool healing SC Attempt. *NOTE: Applies to the Healing Attempt, NOT to the Healing Results.*

20. **Player's Choice:** The player chooses from any of the other options on the chart above.

STEP 3A (OPTIONAL) - Assign additional Backgrounds & Traits

This is an Optional step for Backgrounds & Character Traits. Once you have rolled for your first (mandatory) background or trait in Step 3, you can choose to add more Backgrounds or Traits to your character. Each listed Background or Trait is either a PERK or FLAW, and each has at least one point level assigned to it. **Perks** are generally positive backgrounds, while **Flaws** are generally negative backgrounds for your character. Perks and Flaws offset each other.

Your character is considered to have a ZERO value (the rolled Background or Trait counts as ZERO). You can add as many Backgrounds and Traits as you desire, but the total point level must be equal to, or less than, ZERO when you are done. In other words, if you add three (3) points worth of Perks, you must add at least three (3) points worth of Flaws. You can always end up with more Flaws than Perks, but never more Perk points. One last consideration is that Backgrounds and Traits may NOT be chosen more than once unless specifically allowed in the description.

The lists below are divided into Perks and Flaws and arranged further by point value and alphabetically for ease of use.

NOTE: The effects of the Backgrounds & Traits listed below may differ from the similar Backgrounds or Traits listed above. Any extra Backgrounds & Traits chosen will compound with the initially rolled Background or Trait.

Perks
The perks listed below are generally considered positive enhancements to the character.

Value	Perk	Value	Perk
1	Animal Empathy	2	Quick Healer
1	Extremely Attractive	3	Everyman
1	Team Player	3	Innate Direction
2	Acute Perception	3	Hardy
2-4	Ambidextrous	3-5	Wealthy
2	Charming	4	Eidetic Memory
2	Famous	4	Extremely Graceful
2	Fervent	4	Extremely Lucky
2-4	Political Influence	4	Sixth Sense

Animal Empathy - 1 Point PERK: The character has a natural affinity for working with and befriending natural, relatively unintelligent animals. This does not apply to "unnatural" or Incursion-based creatures such as dragons or griffons (any creature which can be classified as a "monster" will not be affected by this ability – GM discretion) or Others. The character gains a (+4) permanent modifier to **Survival: Taming**.

Extremely Attractive - 1 Point PERK: Your character is incredibly good-looking. They gain a (+3) permanent modifier to the **Influence** skill. *NOTE: You cannot take this with Attractive, Ugly, or Extremely Ugly.*

Team Player - 1 Point PERK: This character is especially good at working with others and creating an environment, which encourages others to excel during team efforts. A character with this Perk will cause all members of the party to gain (+2) conditional modifier to all actions when they coordinate their actions and work together. Characters who are not participating in the team effort will not receive the bonus. The GM has discretion on when these situations apply. If a member of the group has the **Lone Gunman** flaw they will not receive this bonus and their negative modifier will cancel out any benefits gained by this ability if they participate in the team activity.

Acute Perception - 2 Point PERK: The character is very perceptive, seeing and hearing what is happening. The character gains a (+5) permanent modifier to the **Survival: Awareness** proficiency.

Ambidextrous - 2 or 4 Point PERK: Normally, characters have only one hand/side that is dominant. This is the hand that they write with, eat with, and fight with while using one-handed melee or ranged weapons. Any off-hand use normally receives a (-15) conditional modifier to actions. Ambidextrous allows a character to use both hands.

- 2 Point PERK: Character only negates part of the modifier, making off-hand use a (-5) conditional modifier instead of the normal (-15) conditional modifier.
- 4 Point PERK: Character totally negates the off-hand penalty, and allows them to wield two one-handed weapons with no penalties for offhand use.

Charming - 2 Point PERK: The character is very charismatic when they communicate with others. They gain a (+3) permanent modifier to the **Influence** skill.

Famous - 2 Point PERK: The character is famous, and their name is known throughout the region for a specific reason. The character gains a (+3) permanent modifier to the **Influence** skill, and they receive a (-10) conditional modifier to any attempts to hide or blend in with the crowd. *NOTE: The player suggests the reason and scope of the character's "fame". The GM has final approval. NOTE: Player may not take Famous with Notoriety, Infamous, or Notorious without GM approval.*

Fervent - 2 Point PERK: This Trait allows your character to heal their Soul Pool at a much more rapid rate. They gain a (+2) conditional modifier to any Soul Pool healing SC Results. *NOTE: Applies to the Healing Results, NOT to the Healing Attempts.*

Political Influence - 2-4 Point PERK: The character has political influence at the local, state, or federal level.

- 2 Point PERK: This character can contact and attempt to sway local-level politicians. The character gains a (+3) conditional modifier to **Influence** attempts with local-level political figures.
- 3 Point PERK: This character can contact and attempt to sway local and state-level politicians. The character gains a (+5) conditional modifier to **Influence** attempts with local and state-level political figures.
- 4 Point PERK: This character can contact and attempt to sway local, state, and federal-level politicians, and the character gains a (+7) conditional modifier to **Influence** attempts with local, state, and federal-level political figures.

Quick Healer - 2 Point PERK: This Trait allows your character to heal at a much more rapid rate. The character gains a (+2) conditional modifier to any Life Pool healing SC Results. *NOTE: Applies to the Healing Results, NOT to the Healing Attempt. This Trait cannot be taken with either version of the Slow Healer Trait.*

Everyman - 3 Point PERK: This Perk allows the character to blend into the crowd. They simply look "bland" and are able to be overlooked while in a crowd. The character gains a (+10) conditional modifier to **Survival: Stealth** action while trying to blend into a crowd. *NOTE: This cannot be taken with Notoriety, Famous, Infamous, or Notorious.*

Innate Direction - 3 Point PERK: This character always knows the compass directions. It doesn't matter whether they are underground or above ground, they always know which direction is which. This character gains a (+10) permanent modifier to both **Survival: Maps** and **Transport: Navigation**.

Hardy - 3 Point PERK: This trait allows a character to resist disease, infection, and toxins much better than other characters. This character gains a (+5) conditional modifier to **HEA** SCs, including being infected with Therianthropy and Vampire/Vampyre infections.

Wealthy - 3-5 Point PERK: The character handles wealth well. This character has either inherited sizable wealth or has learned to handle their wealth to build it up until now.

- 3 Point PERK: This character gains **Wealth** (+2). The character also gains a (+3) conditional modifier for **Influence: Negotiation** skill when negotiating to purchase or sell something, or for negotiating wages.
- 4 Point PERK: This character gains **Wealth** (+3). The character also gains a (+5) conditional modifier for **Influence: Negotiation** skill when negotiating to purchase or sell something, or for negotiating wages.
- 5 Point PERK: This character gains **Wealth** (+5). The character gains a (+10) conditional modifier for **Influence: Negotiation** skill when negotiating to purchase or sell something, or for negotiating their wages.

Eidetic Memory - 4 Point PERK: This character has eidetic memory (commonly called "Photographic Memory"), and can remember specific details about what they have read or seen. Because they remember almost everything they read or see, the character gains a (+20) permanent modifier to **Knowledge** skill because their memory is so vast.

Extremely Graceful - 4 Point PERK: The character is graceful. The character gains a (+2) permanent modifier to the **HEC** attribute (maximum HEC rank maximum for the character's attribute - "20" for humans).

Extremely Lucky - 4 Point PERK: This character is extremely lucky. This character gains a (+7) permanent modifier to the character's **LCK** attribute (maximum LCK rank is the maximum for the character's attribute - "20" for humans).

Sixth Sense - 4 Point PERK: This character can faintly sense when they are going to be attacked. They gain a (+20) conditional modifier to **Passive Defense** OCs.

FLAWS

The Flaws below are generally considered detrimental to the development of the character.

Value	Flaw	Value	Flaw
1-4	Allergies	2	Easily Surprised
1	Insomniac	2	Extremely Ugly
1	Nervous Tic	2-4	High Debt Load
1	Oath Bound	2	Lone Gunman
1	Obsessive / Compulsive	2	Notorious
1	Orphaned	2-4	Paranoia
1-3	Phobia	2	Slow Healer
1-10	Scars / Disfigurement	2	Stutter / Stammer
1-2	Sheltered	2-4	Wanted Criminal
1-4	Specific Addiction	2	Weak Immune System
2	ADOS	2	Zealot
2	Apathetic	3	Diseased
2	Apostate of Faith	3	Extremely Clumsy
2	Conspiracy Theorist	3	Extremely Unlucky
2	Convicted Criminal	3	Hangry
2	Directionally Challenged	4	Loss of Sight or Hearing
2-4	Duty or Favor		

Allergies - 1-4 Point FLAW: The character has allergies to specific things or environmental conditions. The player and GM decide what the specific allergen is.

- 1 Point FLAW: The character has a minor allergic reaction to a specific thing or a specific environmental condition. The character receives a (-2) modifier to all actions when the condition is present unless controlled by medicine or allergen removal.
- 4 Point FLAW: This character's allergic reaction to a specific item or substance is very severe. If exposed to the substance, the character has a severe reaction that might require medical attention. After medical attention (or faith healing) is applied, the character receives a (-10) modifier to all actions for (30 - HEA) hours.

Insomniac - 1 Point FLAW: A character with this trait is unable to get good rest at night, and therefore they are constantly tired and cranky. This character receives a (-2) permanent modifier to the **Influence** skill.

Nervous Tic - 1 Point FLAW: The character has a repetitive movement or gesture when nervous, which makes all other characters feel uncomfortable. The character receives a (-2) permanent modifier to the **Influence** skill.

Oath Bound - 1 Point FLAW: This character has sworn a deep, blood oath regarding something non-trivial. Any actions that go directly against the oath receive a (–10) conditional modifier. Most non-combat actions that will directly support the oath gain a (+5) conditional modifier. *NOTE: The player suggests the oath and recommends how it may affect the character. The GM has final approval and has discretion on the actions which he determines go against and support the oath.*

Obsessive / Compulsive - 1 Point FLAW: The character tends to obsess over one or more facets of their life, and will carry that to an extreme to complete their goals. Such a character must make a JDG SC (Target 20) to abstain from participating in Obsessive/ Compulsive behavior (such as the need to clean a dirty area) when they do not wish to give in. If the character fails the roll the character will receive a (–10) conditional modifier to all OC/SC attempts until they either complete the required actions to meet the Obsessive/Compulsive need or are removed from the situation for at least 1 hour. The GM works with the player to define the Obsessive/Compulsive triggers.

Orphaned - 1 Point FLAW: The character was an orphan as a child. This character receives a (-5) conditional modifier to any situation that involves trusting institutional leaders. This character also gains a (+5) permanent modifier to the **Survival: Forage** skill.

Phobia - 1-3 Point FLAW: The character has a fear or phobia of a specific condition. This can be an item, organism, being, place, or other things. NOTE: This should be something that is POSSIBLE to encounter. For instance, it would generally not be acceptable to have a phobia of "Living Dinosaurs" (unless, of course, they REALLY want the GM to accept that challenge).

- 1 Point FLAW: Minor Phobia – The character receives a (-2) conditional modifier to all SCs and OCs while that condition is present. If more than one phobia-inducing situation is present then add all the appropriate modifiers together, and then double the total. This Trait may be chosen more than once, each being a separate Phobia.
- 3 Point FLAW: Major Phobia – The character receives a (-5) conditional modifier to all SCs and OCs while that condition is present. If more than one phobia-inducing situation is present then add all the appropriate modifiers together, and then double the total. This Trait may be chosen more than once, each being a separate Phobia.

Scars/Disfigurement - 1-10 Point FLAW: This character has had a rough and adventurous life, is really clumsy, or is really unfortunate. They have disfigurements ranging from scarring to deformities, or even amputations. NOTE: This Flaw cannot be taken with the perks Attractive or Extremely Attractive.

- 1 Point FLAW: The character has pretty extensive visible scarring, either on their limbs or even on their torso/neck. The character receives a (-1) permanent modifier to **Influence: Performance**.
- 3 Point FLAW: The character has extensive visible scarring, especially covering part of their neck and up into their face. The character receives a (-3) permanent modifier to **Influence: Performance**.
- 5 Point FLAW: The character has a disfigurement on one of their hands or one of their feet Choose either hand or foot, and then define which one. If the character chooses a hand disfigurement, the character receives a (-2) permanent modifier to **HEC** (minimum "1"). If the character chooses a foot disfigurement, the character receives a (-2) permanent modifier to **QCK** (minimum "1"). *NOTE: These modifiers apply even if the character has or is able to use prosthetic devices.*
- 7 Point FLAW: The character has a serious disfigurement with one of their limbs. This may be a genetic limb difference from birth or amputation due to medical necessity. Choose either an arm or a leg, and then define which one. If the character chooses an arm, the character receives a (-5) permanent modifier to **HEC** (minimum "1"). If the character chooses a leg, the character receives a (-5) permanent modifier to **QCK** (minimum "1"). *NOTE: These modifiers apply even if the character has or is able to use prosthetic devices.*
- 10 Point FLAW: The character has multiple limbs with limb difference/limb disfigurement/amputation. Choose at least two limbs to have the disfigurement. For each arm chosen, the character receives a (-7) permanent modifier to **HEC**. For each leg chosen, the character receives a (-7) permanent modifier to **QCK**. The character can choose both arms, both legs, or one or more of each. *NOTE: The modifiers apply even if the character has or is able to use prosthetic devices. Specific prosthetic devices may offset or partially offset the penalties due to their design.*

Sheltered - 1-2 Point FLAW: This character led a sheltered life throughout their early years. Their parents/guardians were strict about what they did, with whom they gathered, and what media they consumed.

- 1 Point FLAW: This character was sheltered during their early years. This character receives a (-2) permanent modifier to the **Influence** skill.
- 2 Point FLAW: This character was much more sheltered. This character receives a (-3) permanent modifier to the **Influence** skill.

Specific Addiction - 1-4 Point FLAW: This character is addicted to a substance (such as alcohol or drugs) or an event (such as theft, thrill-seeking, or shopping). When exposed to the substance/event, the character must roll a JDG SC with a Target Number of 15 ((+5) per point of Addiction) to stop themselves from over-indulging. This Trait may be chosen more than once, each being a separate Addiction. The player works with the GM to determine the addiction and scope of the Addiction. For instance, if the character has a 2-point Addiction, the JDG SC would be 15 + 5 + 5 = 25.

ADOS - Attention Deficit, Ooooh Shiny! - 2 Point FLAW: The character has problems focusing on any one event for more than a short time, and constantly wants to be doing something. This character will not be very patient, often precipitating action just for action's sake. The character will receive a (-5) conditional modifier for any non-exciting or non-Combat actions lasting longer than 10 minutes.

Apathetic - 2 Point FLAW: Your character takes an incredibly long time to heal their Soul Pool. The character receives a (-2) conditional modifier to any Soul Pool healing SC Results. *NOTE: Applies to Healing Results, NOT to the Healing Attempts.*

Apostate of Faith - 2 Point FLAW: The character is an Apostate of their Faith. This means that they no longer believe in their original Faith. This does not mean that they cannot gain Faith or regain their Faith, however, the character receives a (-10) conditional modifier to any **Faith**-based skill until they restore or gain Faith.

Conspiracy Theorist - 2 Point FLAW: This character is a conspiracy theorist. They see conspiracies everywhere, even when there are none to be found. This carries a social stigma, as the character will often monologue their pet theories to anyone who will listen. This character receives a (-3) permanent modifier to the **Influence** skill. The character also receives an additional (-5) conditional modifier to **Influence: Negotiation** when dealing with any government officials due to hostility.

Convicted Criminal - 2 Point FLAW: This character is a Convicted Criminal. They were convicted of some crime(s) and served their time. This status carries a social stigma that makes it difficult to find employment, and they are not allowed to participate in elections or find employment with regular military or law enforcement units – with very few exceptions – within the jurisdiction/country where they were convicted. This character also receives a (-10) conditional modifier to the **Influence** skill when dealing with the military, law enforcement, or governmental employees from the original arresting agency, and a (-5) conditional modifier to the **Influence** skill when dealing with all other military, law enforcement, or governmental employees. The player recommends the crime, time, and agency/jurisdiction for GM approval.

Directionally Challenged - 2 Point FLAW: This character tends to get lost very easily. The character receives a (-5) permanent modifier to **Survival: Maps** and **Transport: Navigation**.

Duty or Favor - 2-4 Point FLAW: The character owes a debt, duty, or major favor to a person or organization. The "duty" or "favor" is typically the result of serving with and giving loyalty to a particular organization, like a military unit, business, or even a criminal organization, and the character consequently feels that they owe a "debt" in return to the organization. The favor may be to an individual or an organization. This is not a monetary amount owed but instead is a "debt, favor, or duty" that the organization or person will collect when they need to. This can happen a long time after the original debt, and at inopportune times. The character will risk retaliation if they do not fulfill the debt when asked, and the character would usually rather suffer (and even die if the debt is enough) rather than betray that organization.

This flaw may be chosen more than once, although each choice must be a different Duty or Favor to a different person/organization.

- 2 Point FLAW: The character's debt is a "small" debt that may require the character to look the other way, or to provide certain information at certain times. This debt is not going to come up often, and the "requests" will seem relatively small. This type of debt usually arises from serving with or for the organization for such a length of service that the character feels a loyalty or duty to the organization/person.
- 3 Point FLAW: This character's debt is a "large" debt that will require the character to be more active in helping out the organization or person, and will come up more often. Like the "small" debt, this debt will not usually cause the character to directly take action to support the organization.
- 4 Point FLAW: This character's debt is a "giant" debt that will forever place the character in the debt of the organization or person, and require the character to actively support the organization or person's goals at key times. This type of debt is usually an intense loyalty.

NOTE: The player makes suggestions for both the original debt and the organization or person that provided the debt. The GM has final approval and determination of value.

Easily Surprised - 2 Point FLAW: This disadvantage means that your character is very easily surprised. They receive a (-5) conditional modifier to any **Passive Defense** OCs.

Extremely Ugly - 2 Point FLAW: Your character is hideous to look at. They receive a (-3) permanent modifier to the **Influence** skill. *NOTE: The character cannot take this with Attractive, Extremely Attractive, or Ugly.*

High Debt Load - 2-4 Point FLAW: This flaw means that the character owes a tremendous amount of debt, either from their own mistakes and choices, or they have inherited their high debt load from their parents or family.

- 2 Point FLAW: This level means that the character's debt has piled up and that traditional loans are very difficult to get. The character receives **Wealth** (-3). This requires constant upkeep, and the character receives a (-5) conditional modifier to any **Influence** SC or OC for monetary discussions.
- 3 Point FLAW: This level means that the character has several creditors actively searching for them and that traditional and high-risk loans are near impossible to get. This character receives **Wealth** (-4). This requires constant upkeep, and any stable, non-criminal job will have its wages garnished. The character receives a (-7) conditional modifier to any **Influence** SCs or OCs for monetary discussions.
- 4 Point FLAW: This level means that the character has filed for bankruptcy, and all non-criminal loans are impossible to get, and criminal-backed loans come with a steep price. The character receives a **Wealth** (-5). The character receives a (-10) conditional modifier to any **Influence** SC or OC for monetary discussions.

Lone Gunman - 2 Point FLAW: A Lone Gunman does not do well at working with others and when they do their attitude creates an environment that causes others to stress. This character is generally unpleasant to work with and typically keep to themselves. A character with this background will receive a (-10) conditional modifier when **Working Together** on any skill. For more information, see Working Together in the *Hidden Worlds Refined Core*, Chapter Three, Playing the Game.

Notorious - 2 Point FLAW: This character has a very bad reputation that is known throughout the region. The character gains a (+5) conditional modifier to the **Influence** skill when dealing with a criminal element. They also receive a (-15) conditional modifier to any attempts to hide or blend in with the crowd. *NOTE: The player makes suggestions for the reason and scope of the character's "infamy". The GM has final approval. GM NOTE: Players may not take Notorious with Notoriety, Infamous, or Famous without GM approval.*

Paranoia - 2-4 Point FLAW: This character believes that certain factors or beings are actively working against them, and will often see connections in the most unlikely places - whether those connections truly exist or not.

- 2 Point FLAW: Minor Paranoia – This character receives a (-4) permanent modifier to **Influence: Leadership** and **Influence: Negotiation**. They also gain a (+4) conditional modifier to see through an **Influence: Deception** OC, when they are the target of the Influence: Deception attempt.
- 4 Point FLAW: Major Paranoia – This character receives a (-10) permanent modifier to **Influence: Leadership** and **Influence: Negotiation**. They also gain a (+10) conditional modifier to see through an **Influence: Deception** OC, when they are the target of the Influence: Deception attempt.

Slow Healer - 2 Point FLAW: Your character takes an incredibly long time to heal. The character receives a (-8) conditional modifier to any Life Pool healing SC Attempt. *NOTE: Applies to Healing Attempt, NOT to the Healing Results. This Trait cannot be taken with either version of the Quick Healer Trait.*

Stutter / Stammer - 2 Point FLAW: The character has problems speaking in a clear and concise manner. The character receives a (-4) permanent modifier to **Influence: Performance** and **Influence: Negotiation** skills.

Wanted Criminal - 2-4 Point FLAW: The character is currently wanted for a crime by authorities. This flaw may be chosen more than once, although each choice must be a different option for a different crime.

- 2 Point FLAW: This character is running from local authorities that want them for a crime worth (d20) months in jail/prison. While the character is "Wanted," the Character receives a (-5) conditional modifier for the **Influence** skill when dealing with any level of law enforcement.
- 3 Point FLAW: This character is running from state authorities that are looking for them for a crime worth (d20/2) years in prison. While the character is "Wanted," the Character receives a (-10) conditional modifier for the **Influence** skill when dealing with any level of law enforcement.
- 4 Point FLAW: This character is running from federal authorities that are looking for them for a crime worth (2d20) years in prison. If you roll a "1" on either roll, your character is wanted for a capital offense. While the character is "Wanted," the Character receives a (-15) conditional modifier for the **Influence** skill when dealing with any level of law enforcement.

NOTE: The player works with the GM to determine both the crime and the jurisdiction/locality of the crime.

Weak Immune System - 2 Point FLAW: This means the character has a weak constitution and gets sick easily. The character receives a (-5) conditional modifier to **HEA** OCs for disease, infection, and toxins.

Zealot - 2 Point FLAW: This character is a Zealot for their chosen cause. The player chooses the issue, and they have an extreme passion for that issue. The character gains a (+5) conditional modifier for all actions that relate directly to the chosen zealotry, and a (-10) conditional modifier for any actions that directly conflict with their Zealotry (GM Discretion applies). This zealotry applies to all situations, and the character can, and will, often offend others with the pursuit of their zealotry. If two choices are offered, the character should consistently choose the option that further benefits their crusade.

Diseased - 3 Point FLAW: This character suffers from an incurable, but not necessarily fatal, disease. While it is not contagious, or even necessarily visible, they do have a self-imposed social stigma on them. The character receives a (-5) permanent modifier to the **Influence** skill, as well as a **Wealth** (-1) due to medical upkeep. *NOTE: The player works with the GM to determine disease/condition particulars.*

Extremely Clumsy - 3 Point FLAW: The character is extremely clumsy. The character receives a (-2) permanent modifier to their **HEC** attribute.

Extremely Unlucky - 3 Point FLAW: The character is extremely Unlucky. The character receives a (-4) permanent modifier to the **LCK** Attribute.

Hangry - 3 Point FLAW: When this character is hungry, they get angry. The character must have food at regular meal-time intervals and snacks in between. If they go more than three hours without some form of food or snack, they must make a HEA SC (Target 25). For every hour after the first roll, the character must make the same HEA SC attempt, with the target number increasing by (+5) for each additional attempt.

If the character fails any of the rolls, they receive a (-5) conditional modifier to JDG and all JDG-based skills, and they also receive a (-2) conditional modifier to ALR and all ALR-based skills except the **Negotiation: Intimidation** Expertise. They also gain a (+5) conditional modifier to **Negotiation: Intimidation** Expertise. The Hangry condition and modifiers last until the character has a full meal.

Loss of Sight or Hearing - 4 Point FLAW: The character does not have the use of one of the following senses: sight or hearing. The character receives a (-15) permanent modifier to **Survival: Awareness**, which becomes a (-60) conditional modifier if the character is relying solely on that lost sense for the SC or OC.

STEP 3B (OPTIONAL) – ROLL FOR CONTACTS/FRIENDS/ENEMIES (CFE)

The CFE Roll starts your character with some contacts, friends, and enemies. These are people or Others that your character knows before they start the game, all based on their history.

Contacts are NPCs that your character knows, and that know your character. While they would not be classified as friends, they may be a source of information or very minor assistance, as long as it does not jeopardize the Contact in any way.

Friends are NPCs that your character is very familiar with. They will often assist the character with information or other assistance, as long as the risks are not too great. Friends are a reliable source of help at most times.

Enemies are NPCs that are actively hostile to your character. This may range from minor annoyances (like a good friend's spouse) all the way up to someone that is actively trying to harm or thwart your character.

The CFE Roll is designed to give your character a history and story, as well as provide potential interactions during gameplay. Interpret the results below in a way that would fit your character's background and history.

Roll of 1

- Contact: Former high school classmate in a decent job.
- Friend: Drinking buddy friend who is a former co-worker.
- Enemies: Local police chief hates your character because your character dated, and then dumped, their child. The County judge dislikes your character. A Poltergeist is attached to an object that is important to your character and is in your possession, and the poltergeist doesn't like you.

Roll a 2

- Contacts: Your character is in good standing with the local fraternal organization (think Lions, Kiwanis, VFW, etc.)
- Friends: Good Friend who is mid-level in local law enforcement, like a lieutenant or sergeant. A good friend at mid-level in the town hall in a non-elected position.
- Enemies: Two or three hostile ex-significant others generally make themselves a nuisance.

Roll a 3

- Contacts: Contact in the local mayor's office – not the mayor, but someone on the staff. Your character is well-known at a local bar/restaurant (Norm!).
- Friends: One really good high school friend, they stayed close, and they have significant contacts in particular state business associations. One good friend who is your character's normal drinking/fishing/recreation/hobby companion.
- Enemy: Spouse of the good friend who is your character's normal drinking/fishing/recreation/hobby – they really do not like your character.

Roll a 4

- Contacts: Contacts in the regional FBI office, including at least one Special Agent.
- Friend: Friend of a local mid-level mafia guy, like a lieutenant or other "made" person.
- Enemy: Low-level local mafia guy in the same outfit as your character's friend, is jealous of the access the character has to their friend.

Roll a 5

- Contacts: Multiple contacts at the state-level Prosecutor's office, including the state Attorney General.
- Friend: Friend with a local LEO (beat cop).
- Enemies: Local IRS agent is suspicious of your character's activities/life, so they make a nuisance of themselves. A local police captain has complete disdain for your character because they think your character is a terrible influence on their son or daughter or other family.

Roll a 6

- Contact: Your character is the "phone-a-friend" for the town drunk when they get harassed/arrested.
- Friends: Your character is friends with their old college frat/sorority, or equivalent, leaving them with several people they call friends.
- Enemy: The Dean of your character's alma mater despises your character.

Roll a 7

- Contacts: Your character knows a lot of contacts at their local Religious organization/church.
- Friend: Your character's Best Friend from high school is still their friend, although they hold a menial position at their employment.
- Enemies: Your character has a very bad reputation with a local news organization.

Roll an 8

- Contact: Low-level contact at a local news organization.
- Friends: Friends with both the local arson investigator and the fire chief of the local department.
- Enemies: A couple of the mid-level local law enforcement officers, like lieutenants or sergeants, really do not like your character.

Roll a 9

- Contact: Your character knows a tabloid reporter/photographer.
- Friend: Good college friend is a producer for a national news media company.
- Enemy: National on-air talent in the same media company as your character's good college friend is suspicious of your character and their relationship with the producer.

Roll a 10

- Contacts: First-name basis with the staff at a local hobby-related store.
- Friend: Friends with the local crime-beat reporters (print and tv).
- Enemies: Your character has been targeted by a local-level gang/clan of Others, like gremlins, gnomes, or fairies.

Roll an 11

- Contact: Low-level contact with an Other in a local Fae Court.
- Friend: An Other in the SAME Fae Court owes your character a favor and is considered a Friend.
- Enemy: Your character has angered a mid-level Other in an opposing Fae Court.

Roll a 12

- Contact: Contact is a Clerk for a local judge
- Friend: Good friends with a local police detective, who is also a neighbor.
- Enemies: Your character was a witness against local mafia crimes

Roll of 13

- Contact: Contact is the SAC (Special Agent in Command) at the regional FBI or DHS Office.
- Friends: Friends with local therianthrope pack or vampire nest.
- Enemies: Enemies with an opposing therianthrope pack or vampire nest.

Roll of 14

- Contact: Know the Manager at the local hardware or lumber store.
- Friends: Friends with the local building Inspectors.
- Enemy: The Clerk for the city engineer does not like your character.

Roll of 15

- Contact: Know a local beat cop.
- Friends: Friend of an on-air talent, and their spouse, at a national news media company.
- Enemies: Local news media has been scooped by your character to national news media. As a result, the local media outlets do not like your character and will cause problems.

Roll of 16

- Contact: Your character knows someone mid-level at the state Governor's office – someone on staff.
- Friend: Your character is friends with a fae in good standing with one of the Fae Courts.
- Enemies: The opposing Fae Court does not approve of your character's friendship with the opposing fae. They are not hunting for your character, but they just do not like your character.

Roll of 17

- Contacts: Your character knows the top partners at a reputable local law office.
- Friend: Your character has befriended the homeless person sitting outside the law office. They may be more than they appear.
- Enemy: The local beat cop or security guard that tries to run off your character's homeless friend does not like your interference.

Roll of 18

- Contacts: Your character knows the regional SACs for both the FBI and DHS, as well as the Lieutenant at the closest State Police Post.
- Friends: One of the Fae Courts or an equal status (I.e. Vampire Master) owes your character a Favor. Your character is considered Friends of the (entity). For now.
- Enemies: The opposing Fae Court, or opposing powerful entity, disapproves of the status of being owed a favor. They look unfavorably on your character

Roll of 19:

- Contacts: Your character knows a lot of people at a particular national news media organization.
- Friend: Your character was a high school friend with the child of the owner of the said media company, and they remain close.
- Enemy: The media company owner does not approve of your character's friendship with their child.

Roll of 20

- Contacts: Your character has contacts with a fairly large clan of Sasquatch/Bigfoot/Yeti.
- Friend: It turns out your character's best friend from high school is a minor demigod, although they did not really know until after they both graduated. The two remain good friends.
- Enemy: A rival demigod in the same pantheon, but whose parent really does not have much to do with Earth Realm matters, happened to be the person in high school that bullied your character. The bully actually knew they were a demigod at the time.

STEP 4 - ASSIGN AN EDUCATION LEVEL

At this time, choose *one* Education Level for your character. Discuss the details with your GameMaster. Between the two of you, decide on the School name/Location, the cost of attending the school, and the major course of study. You will then recommend the core Skills and Proficiencies that your character would have as a result of their schooling. Once the GM approves of the skill selection, write these details on the character sheet.

NOTE: The Minimum Starting Age listed under each Education Level is the bare minimum that the character starts with after their Education. For instance, if your character has a "High School Graduate" education level, their starting age is "18." Any additional degrees will add to the Minimum Starting Age. Any years in their career would add to that number. **Constructs and most cryptids will not have any formal education based on their background.**

STREET URCHIN

A street urchin has little to no formal schooling at any real level. They are used to a life on the streets and do not react well when put into a classroom or other structured learning environment. It is harder for them to learn, or advance, in Intellect-based skills and proficiencies. This does not mean that they are less intelligent, but that their capacity for learning intellect-based skills is hampered.

Due to their background, a street urchin begins the game with the following **Skills: Survival** (+4), **Survival: Forage** (+2), and **Forage: Urban** Expertise (+4).

Because of their trauma and history, a street urchin character also starts with the **Orphan** Background.

- Starting Wealth Modifier (-4).
- Minimum Starting Age: 12 to 16.

HIGH SCHOOL DROPOUT

This character dropped out of high school early. They did not finish their time in high school, and therefore they did not pick up any extra skills because of it. The high school dropout does begin the game with the Skills **Survival** (+2) and **Knowledge** (+2).

- Starting Wealth Modifier (-2).
- Minimum Starting Age: 16 to 19.

HIGH SCHOOL GRADUATE (HIGH SCHOOL EQUIVALENCY)

The high school graduate worked their way through high school and graduated, but did not go further with their education. Due to their work in high school, the character starts with the following **Skills: Knowledge** (+4), **Electronics** (+2), and (+2) from any one Proficiency from either: **Athletics, Culture, Electronics, Knowledge, Science, or Social**.

- Minimum Starting Age: 18.

COMMUNITY COLLEGE/ASSOCIATE DEGREE/SOME COLLEGE

The character has attended a two-year community-type college, attained their Associate's Degree, or has spent a decent amount of time in a 4-year program at a college. They have not, however, graduated with a traditional 4-year degree like the College Graduate.

The player describes the course of study that their character would pursue, and the GameMaster will approve the program. The Player then suggests the appropriate Core Skills and Proficiencies for that program, getting final approval for the skills from the GM. The character gains the following skills based on the college program: **Knowledge** (+4), **Electronics** (+4), three **Player-Recommended Core** (+4 each), and four **Player-Recommended Proficiencies** (+4 each).

- Starting Wealth Modifier (-1).
- Minimum Starting Age: 20 to 21.

COLLEGE GRADUATE

The college graduate has spent the last several years at college and has graduated with a bachelor's degree in a specific program. The player describes their character's degree program and then suggests the appropriate Core skills and proficiencies for that degree. The character gains the following skills based on the degree program: **Knowledge** (+6), **Electronics** (+4), **Player-Recommended Core** (+15 total, maximum (+5) additional in any Core), and **Player-Recommended Proficiencies** (+20 total, maximum (+7) in any Proficiency).

- Starting Wealth Modifier (-1) to (-2) - based on college choice, GM discretion.
- Minimum Starting Age: 22 to 24.
- *Additional College Graduate Degrees cost (-1) Wealth each.*

Masters-level Degree

The character has graduated from a Masters-level degree program. Like the college degree, the player will suggest the appropriate Core and proficiency skills for the player to choose. The character gains the following skills based on the Master's degree: **Knowledge** (+7), **Electronics** (+4), **Player-Recommended Core** (+17 total–maximum (+7) additional in any Core), **Player-Recommended Proficiencies** (+20 total–maximum (+7) in any Proficiency), and **Player-Recommended Expertise** (+15 total).

- Starting Wealth Modifier (-2) to (-3) - based on college(s) choice, GM discretion.
- Minimum Starting Age: 24 to 26.
- *Additional Masters-Level Degrees cost (-1) Wealth if in a similar field, or (-2) Wealth if not.*
- *NOTE: Expertise ranks should be spent in the degree program that they are choosing.*

Doctorate-level Degree

The character has graduated from a Doctorate-Level program, either an academic (Ph.D.), legal (JD), or medical (MD). As with the college graduate and masters-level degree, the player will suggest the appropriate Core and proficiency skills for the character. The character gains the following skills based on the degree: **Knowledge** (+8), **Electronics** (+5), **Player-Recommended Core** (+18 total–maximum (+7) additional in any Core), **Player-Recommended Proficiencies** (+25 total–maximum (+10) in any Proficiency), and Player-Recommended Expertise (+30 total).

- Starting Wealth (-2) to (-4) - based on college(s) of choice, GM discretion.
- Starting Age - 26 to 28.
- *Additional Doctorate-Level Degrees cost (-2) Wealth if in a similar field, or (-3) Wealth if not.*
- *NOTE: Expertise ranks should be spent in the degree program that they are choosing.*

Once you have decided what education level your character will have, write down the results under the Education Level block on the History Record. Now decide which Core skills and proficiencies your character's education provided. Once the GM has approved your recommendations, choose how many points you want to allocate between those skills.

STEP 5 - Choose the Career(s)

Choose the Career(s) that your character has worked in their lifetime. When you choose the career, figure out the minimum age and minimum education for the career. Consider which skills that career might offer for the character, then list the core skills, and proficiencies of that particular career. Recommend your selections to the GM for their approval.

Career Training: If your character's chosen career has a Career Training component, choose the Duration and Intensity that the Career Training requires. Then refer to the chart below that cross-references the Duration and the Intensity. This will give you the number of Core skills, Proficiencies, and Expertise that your character gains from the training. Those points can then be distributed based on the skills from that training. *NOTE: Skill points gained from Career Training are separate from the skill points gained from the career itself.*

	Short Duration (Less Than 1 Month)	Medium Duration (1-3 Months)	Long Duration (More than 3 Months)
Low Intensity	(+0) Core Skills (+5) Proficiencies (+5) Expertise	(+3) Core Skills (+7) Proficiencies (+10) Expertise	(+5) Core Skills (+10) Proficiencies (+15) Expertise
Medium Intensity	(+3) Core Skills (+7) Proficiencies (+10) Expertise	(+5) Core Skills (+10) Proficiencies (+15) Expertise	(+10) Core Skills (+15) Proficiencies (+20) Expertise
High Intensity	(+5) Core Skills (+10) Proficiencies (+15) Expertise	(+10) Core Skills (+15) Proficiencies (+20) Expertise	(+15) Core Skills (+20) Proficiencies (+30) Expertise

STEP 6 - CHOOSE CAREER LENGTH

The next step is to choose how long your character's career has lasted, at least before the game starts. Choose how long your character has been in their career.

Once you have chosen how long the character has been in their career, refer to the chart below for skills gained during your career. Record the time in your career, and the number of Core, Proficiency, and Expertise points on your character's History Record.

Exception: If the character's ONLY career is Monster Hunter, add (+10) Esoteric core skill, (+15) Proficiency skill points, and (+20) Expertise.

Years	Core	Prof	Exp	Wea	Years	Core	Prof	Exp	Wea
1	+2	+1	–	–	11	+25	+36	+33	+3
2	+7	+3	–	+1	12	+25	+38	+40	+3
3	+15	+7	–	+1	13	+25	+40	+47	+3
4	+19	+11	–	+1	14	+25	+42	+54	+3
5	+22	+18	–	+2	15	+25	+44	+61	+4
6	+24	+24	+5	+2	16	+25	+46	+69	+4
7	+25	+30	+10	+2	17	+25	+48	+75	+4
8	+25	+30	+15	+2	18	+25	+50	+85	+4
9	+25	+32	+21	+2	19	+25	+50	+95	+4
10	+25	+34	+27	+3	20	+25	+50	+100	+5

For each year after the 20th year, add +2 Proficiencies and +7 Expertise.

Take note of how many total years your character has been in their careers. This will become a factor when determining the character's age.

STEP 7 - ROLL FOR CAREER EFFECTS

As the character travels through their career, they sometimes get promotions, add or lose wealth, and occasionally end under terrible, or spectacular, circumstances.

- While working in their career, the character may experience times of greater or lesser Wealth, depending on the circumstances of their work. This is the general average over their entire career. It is the end result, not a measurement per job. Wealth gains and losses may be attributed to job performance (raises) or life events around the career (childbirth or divorce).

- Occasionally a character's career has Ended Well or Ended Badly. This is a story effect that helps inform the player about how their character's career ended. This is a general suggestion for the character's story and history, and the player is free to interpret the result as they wish.

  - If the result shows "Badly," your character's career has ended badly at least once. This might include being fired from the job, ending with a bad lawsuit, or a horrific accident that affected the character. The career ends usually with the Incursion Event (rolled after Passions). If the career "Ended Badly," the character will gain at least one additional Enemy related to their career.
  - If the result shows "Well," your character's career has ended well, usually with high honors and accolades. Your work will be sorry to see you go. If the career "Ended Well," the character will gain at least one additional Friend related to their career.
  - If there is no indication, then the career was generally unremarkable. If the career was generally unremarkable, the character will gain at least one additional Contact related to their career.

- While working in their career, the character will gain either Contacts, Friends, or Enemies related to their career. The relative power of the Contact, Friend, or Enemy is directly proportional to the die roll itself. A low roll will mean a lower-power NPC, while a higher roll means that NPC will have more influence to help, or hurt, the character.

  - Contacts are NPCs that your character knows, and that know your character. While they would not be classified as friends, they may be a source of information or very minor assistance, as long as it does not jeopardize the Contact in any way.
  - Friends are NPCs that your character is very familiar with. They will often assist the character with information or other assistance, as long as the risks are not too great. Friends are a reliable source of help at most times.
  - Enemies are NPCs that are actively hostile to your character. This may range from minor annoyances (like a good friend's spouse) all the way up to someone that is actively trying to harm or thwart your character.

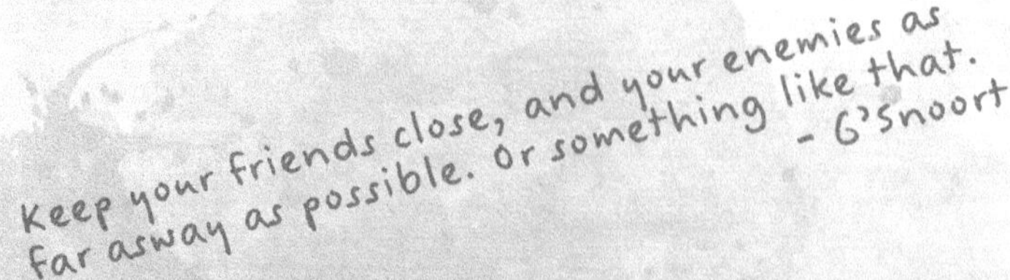

Now, roll a d20 for every career that your character works. Exception: The Monster Hunter Career rolls twice and adds all figures.

Roll	Wealth	Ended	Contacts	Friends	Enemies
1	-2	Badly	–	–	3
2	-2	–	1	–	–
3	-2	Well	–	1	–
4	-1	–	1	–	–
5	-1	Badly	–	–	2
6	-1	Badly	–	–	2
7	–	–	1	–	–
8	–	–	2	–	–
9	–	Well	–	1	–
10	–	–	2	–	–
11	–	Badly	–	–	2
12	–	–	1	–	–
13	–	–	1	–	–
14	–	Badly	–	–	1
15	+1	Well	–	2	–
16	+1	Well	–	2	–
17	+1	–	1	–	–
18	+2	–	2	–	–
19	+2	–	2	–	–
20	+3	Well	–	3	–

STEP 8 - CHOOSE CHARACTER PASSIONS

At this step, choose one or more Passions for your character. Once you have chosen the passion, consult with the GameMaster to determine how much Time your character spends in their pursuit of the passion, and then how much Effort your character will spend in the passion.

One interesting side note to Passions are those Faith-related Passions. The passion may be a study of one particular Faith, or it may be the learning and active practice of casting faith abilities. If the Faith-based Passion is one where they can cast faith abilities, they will gain a number of Faith Abilities based on the Time and Effort that they put into the Passion. For Faith-Based Passions that produce Faith Abilities, refer to Chapter Four, The Power of Faith in the *Hidden Worlds Refined Core*.

When choosing the character's Passion, the player will choose the relative amount of **Time** (Low, Medium, or High) and relative amount of **Effort** (Low, Medium, or High) that the character puts into their Passion.

The character's Time in their Passion is loosely defined as: 1) The amount of time and energy that the character spends to do their Passion, and 2) How long they have been a practitioner of the Passion. The character's Time is characterized into three categories:

- **Low Time:** If the character does not spend much of their time on their Passion or is relatively new to their Passion, they have a Low Time commitment. This does leave them free to have up to two more Low Time passions (a total of three Low Time passions), or they can add a Medium Time passion. If they have a Low Time passion, they cannot also have a High Time passion.

- **Medium Time:** If the character spends a fair amount of their time on their Passion, or has been in their Passion for a while, they have a Medium Time commitment. Their Medium Time passion allows them to add a Low Time passion, however, they cannot add another Medium Time passion. They also cannot add a High Time passion.

- **High Time:** If the character spends a lot of their time on their Passion, and they have spent a long time in their Passion, they have a High Time commitment. If they have a High Time passion, they cannot add any other Passions.

The character's Effort in their Passion is loosely defined as the amount of resources and energy that the character spends to do their Passion. The character's Effort is characterized by three categories:

- **Low Effort:** If the character does not spend much of their resources and energy on their Passion, they have a Low Effort passion. This means the Basic Wealth Cost of this Passion is "0".

- **Medium Effort:** If the character spends a fair amount of their resources and energy on their Passion, they have a Medium Effort passion. This means the Basic Wealth Cost of this Passion is "1".

- **High Effort:** If the character spends a lot of their resources and energy on their Passion, they have a High Effort passion. This means the Basic Wealth Cost of this Passion is "2".

Each Passion has four different factors:

- The Time and Effort spent in a Passion determines how many points the character receives for Core skills, Proficiencies, and Expertise.

- Each Passion has a specific Wealth Cost Modifier. This is based on the equipment, training, and other resources that the passion demands. Training, traveling to participate in the passion, buying equipment or supplies, and taking the time off of work all cost wealth. The Wealth Modifier is added to the base Wealth Cost of the Effort for the character's passion (Rounded-up, Minimum of "1"). For instance, if the Passion is a Medium Effort (Wealth Cost 1), and the Passion's Wealth Modifier is "1", the total Wealth Cost for that Passion would be "2". The character's starting Wealth would be at (-2) due to their passions.

- Each Passion will provide Mechanical and/or Story-based Bonuses based on the pursuit of the character's passion. These are based on what the pursuit of the passion uses or requires, as well as how much Time the character puts into the passion. Time-based bonuses are cumulative. In other words, the bonuses gained from the Low Time passion are added to the listed Medium Time passion, and so on. For instance, if the passion is Low Time, the character may get a smaller, lighter story-based bonus. If the passion is Medium Time, the character would receive the Low Time bonus plus they may get a mid-range mechanical bonus. If the passion is High Time, the character would receive both prior levels and may receive a higher-range story-based bonus and a good mechanical bonus.

- Each Passion will generally come with Starting Equipment appropriate to the pursuit of that passion. Like the mechanical and story-based bonuses, the amount, and quality, of the passion-based equipment are based on the Effort the character puts into their passion. *For instance, if they put Low Effort into their passions, the starting equipment will be less in both quantity and quality. On the other end of the spectrum, If the character puts High Effort into the pursuit of their passion, they would end up with a good amount of high-quality equipment related to their passion.*

Refer to the chart below for the number of Core skills, Proficiencies, and Expertise the character receives from their Passion.

	Low Time Spent (Max. 3 Passions)	Medium Time Spent (Max. 2 Passions)	High Time Spent (Max. 1 Passion)
Low Effort (WEA 0)	(+2) Core Skills (+4) Proficiencies (+1) Expertise	(+4) Core Skills (+8) Proficiencies (+4) Expertise	(+4) Core Skills (+12) Proficiencies (+16) Expertise
Medium Effort (WEA 1)	(+4) Core Skills (+8) Proficiencies (+4) Expertise	(+4) Core Skills (+12) Proficiencies (+16) Expertise	(+4) Core Skills (+18) Proficiencies (+32) Expertise
High Effort (WEA 2)	(+4) Core Skills (+12) Proficiencies (+16) Expertise	(+4) Core Skills (+18) Proficiencies (+32) Expertise	(+8) Core Skills (+24) Proficiencies (+64) Expertise

STEP 9 - CHARACTER AGE STAGE

First, figure out your character's age. Start with their education. This provides the minimum age for a character. Now add the years spent in each of their careers. This total provides the age of your character. For instance, if your character attended college, they will be at least 22 years old. If they then work in their career for 11 years, your character's current age for the game will be 33 years old.

Now refer to the chart below for how that age affects your character. NOTE: Age Stage effects do not compound. Only refer to the current Age Stage that your character fits into. Also **Note:** The years listed for this chart are only valid for uninfected Humans.

CHILD: 0-12 Years Old (*NOTE: Should be Very Rare*)
- The character gains a (-5) permanent modifier to **MIG**, **HEA**, **HEC**, and **JDG** (minimum 1). They also receive a (+3) permanent modifier to **ALR** (maximum based on attribute chart). Also, gain a (-3) permanent modifier to their Life Pool.

TEENAGE: 13-18 Years Old
- This character receives a (+3) permanent modifier to **HEA** and **QCK** (maximum based on attribute chart). They also gain (-3) permanent modifier to **JDG** (minimum 1). They also receive a (+1) permanent modifier to their Life Pool.

YOUNG ADULT: 19-29 Years Old
- No Effects

ADULT: 30-45 Years Old
- The character receives a (+1) permanent modifier to **JDG** and **LCK** (maximum based on attribute chart). They also gain a (-1) permanent modifier to **HEC** and **HEA** (minimum 1).

AGING: 45-65 Years Old
- This character receives a (+2) permanent modifier to **JDG** and **LCK** (maximum based on attribute chart), and a (+1) permanent modifier to **ITL** (maximum based on attribute chart). The character gains a (-1) permanent modifier to **MIG**, **HEC**, **HEA**, and **QCK** (minimum 1).

OLD: 66-90 Years Old
- The character receives a (+3) permanent modifier to **JDG** and **LCK** (maximum based on attribute chart), and a (+1) permanent modifier to **ITL** (maximum based on attribute chart). The character also gains a (-3) permanent modifier to **MIG**, **HEC**, **HEA**, and **QCK** (minimum 1).

ANCIENT: 91-120 Years Old
- The character receives a (+4) permanent modifier to **JDG** and **LCK** (maximum based on attribute chart) and receives a (+2) permanent modifier to **ITL** (maximum based on attribute chart). The character also gains a (-5) permanent modifier to **MIG**, **HEC**, **HEA**, and **QCK** (minimum 1).

STEP 10 - CHARACTER BODY TYPE

Your character's Body Type is simply a descriptor for their Height and Weight. As with most of the other mechanical systems in *Hidden Worlds*, these descriptions are intended as guidelines, not absolute numbers. The character's Body Type is a loose way to gauge your character's general physicality.

Begin by choosing your character's **Height**. Like the Curve system, there are no concrete numbers attached to the height of the character, only generalities. The height of the character may provide certain modifiers.

DWARF: The character is incredibly short, well under five feet tall, and even sometimes shorter than four feet. Typically formed from a genetic condition, the character has typically had to deal with the condition for their entire life.
- The character gains a (-2) permanent modifier to **QCK** (minimum 1).

SHORT: The character is shorter than most people, usually no taller than around five feet tall. This usually results in teasing as they grow up, often leading to sensitivity to comments made about their height.
- The character gains a (-1) permanent modifier to **QCK** (minimum 1).

AVERAGE: The character is of average height, usually somewhere between five and six feet tall.
- No effects.

TALL: The character is taller than average. Ending up taller than six feet in height, they are sometimes teased, and they often have to duck around low ceilings, doorways, and lights.
- The character receives a (+1) permanent modifier to **QCK** (maximum based on attribute chart).

GIANT: The character is incredibly tall, towering over others at something around or over seven feet tall. Growing up, they got teased for their height and likely developed sensitivity to those kinds of comments.
- The character receives a (+1) permanent modifier to **QCK** (maximum based on attribute chart). Receive a (+5) conditional modifier to **Social: Negotiation** when purposefully being intimidating.

Now write down your character's height category on the Character Record Sheet, and note any effects or modifiers.

Next, you will choose your character's basic **Weight** category. Like the character's height, there are no definitive numbers given, as the numbers would rely on the character's height and other factors. There may be effects and modifiers for your character due to their weight.

GAUNT: The character is gaunt to the point of sickly. With no extra fat and no real muscle definition, they look extremely undernourished. They weigh a lot less than the average person for their height.
- The character gains a (-2) permanent modifier to **HEA** (minimum 1).

SKINNY: The character is skinny. While they have no real extra fat on their body, they may have some muscle tone. They weigh less than the average person of their height.
- The character gains a (-1) permanent modifier to **HEA** (minimum 1).

AVERAGE: This character is around the average weight and build for a person of their height. They have no problem finding clothing or equipment in their size.
  • No Effects.

HEAVY: This character is heavier than the average character for their height. Their build may range from stocky to overweight.
  • The character receives a (-1) permanent modifier to **HEA** (maximum based on attribute chart), and they gain an additional (-1) permanent modifier to their Life Pool.

OBESE: The character is very overweight for a person of their height. Their build is very large and may include a distended stomach or large rolls of fat on their appendages.
  • The character gains a (-2) permanent modifier to **HEA** (minimum 1) and an additional (-4) permanent modifier to Life Pool.

STEP 11: You ARE the Incursion Event

As a Created Other, your character is their own Incursion Event.

STEP 12 - Choose Character Starting Equipment

Starting Equipment is based on starting Wealth and careers and passions. Compile and present a REASONABLE list of equipment for your character to start with. When completing your character's equipment list, there are a few things to keep in mind.

Clothing

Your character should start with at least a basic wardrobe that is appropriate to their wealth, career, and passions. This should include the clothing that they wear to work, that they wear on a daily basis, and even specialty clothing from their work and passions (as such applies). This applies to footwear (shoes) as well as jewelry or other accessories. You should also consider outerwear, such as coats and inclement weather gear. Consider where they store their wardrobe and how much clothing they might have.

Equipment

Your character should have the equipment that is appropriate for their careers and passions. Considering the character's wealth as a limiting factor, start with listing equipment from the character's career. If the character is a businessperson, having a computer and other personal electronics are very appropriate for the equipment list. If your character also has passions that take them hiking or camping outdoors, then a first aid kit, a tent, and various camping materials are also appropriate.

Consider carefully where the character stores their equipment. They will only have their equipment available at appropriate times—the character would not likely have their expensive laptop while camping, and they would not likely have their tent while working. Even if detailed on the sheet, the character will generally only have access to appropriate equipment at appropriate times.

WEAPONS AND ARMOR

Any weapons or armor that your character has should be appropriate to their careers or passions. Considering your character's wealth as a limiting factor, and their passion Effort, if any in the appropriate area, choose carefully what kind of weapons your character might own. Those weapons include modern or antique firearms, knives, and other bladed weapons, bows and crossbows, hunting weapons, and exotic or ancient weapons. *NOTE: This game is in a modern setting, and your character should only start with weapons that make sense to their story.*

If your character starts with weapons, they may also need equipment that goes along with the weapons. Bladed weapons usually require scabbards or sheaths, and pistols usually require holsters or some method of carrying them. You may also want to consider if the weapon requires any special ammunition or equipment to care for them. And as above, there will likely be times that your character may not have access to their firearms.

With regards to armor, your character should have a VERY good reason to own armor during character creation. Careers in Law Enforcement would certainly provide body armor, and a career in security or armored cars might provide one as well. Other than that, not very many characters will start with body armor/bullet-resistant vest.

When you have your character's weapons and/or armor approved, the stats can be found in the Section called Equipment: Weapons.

NOTE: Nothing in character creation precludes characters from obtaining weapons and/or armor during story play.

LIVING ARRANGEMENTS

Consider your character's wealth when establishing your character's living arrangements. Does your character's wealth justify a small apartment or a large, lavish home? Consider the location of the living space as well, taking into account careers and passions, and storage issues.

REASONABLE

The key to making this equipment list work is to make sure it is reasonable. Consult with the GM and make sure that they approve of your list. Ask them if there is anything else that they would suggest, based on your character's background, careers, and passions. Also, ask them if there is anything they want your character to have based on the upcoming campaign.

As a final note, remember that the GM has the final discretion for your character's equipment list.

Reasonable? Yeah.
Tell that to Nate...
– G'Snoort

STEP 13 - FIGURE YOUR CHARACTER'S WEALTH

As discussed in the chapter about The Curve, Hidden Worlds has a Wealth system. The character's Wealth is a general measure of their lifestyle, their purchasing power, and their affluence. During Character Creation, the characters start with a baseline "Middle Class" value for their wealth. This value of "10" is then affected by several of the next steps in character creation.

Backgrounds & Traits, Education, Life Path, Career Path, and Passions all have possibilities of affecting a character's Wealth. At this point, add (or subtract) all the WEA from those items, add (+10) and that is your character's current Wealth.

STEP 14 - CHARACTER'S TALENTS AND OTHER NOTES

Each playable Other gains special abilities and bonuses due to their "Otherness". These are called Talents. In this next step, you will find your character's Other type, and then note down the character's Talents and any other notes and bonuses that they receive as a Created Other. *NOTE: Unless otherwise noted, Talent use requires a Standard Action.*

DHAMPIR

The Dhampir receives three Talents:

Feed the Monster
- Roll a JDG SC (Target 20). Costs (-5) Soul Pool.
- When the dhampir unleashes their inner monster, they gain a massive energy boost for (10) rounds. The dhampir gains a (+10) conditional modifier to **HEC**, **QCK**, and **MIG**, as well as their related skills. The dhampir also receives a (-10) conditional modifier to **JDG**, **ALR**, and **ITL**, as well as the related skills, for the same amount of time.

Hunter's Senses
- Roll a JDG SC (Target 10). Costs (-1) Soul Pool.
- When the dhampir heightens their senses, they become much more perceptive for 10 minutes. The dhampir gains low light vision (black and white). They also gain a (+10) conditional modifier to any **Survival: Awareness** SC or OC.

Heal the Monster
- When a dhampir drinks enough fresh blood, they can heal their Life Pool. When they feed on the blood, they gain (+20) Life Pool (up to their maximum). They can drink blood to gain the Life Pool once every ten minutes.
- When they drink blood, they risk becoming addicted to the euphoria from the feeding. If they drink blood too often (too many times per day), the GM may have the dhampir make a JDG SC (Target 30). If they fail, they gain a permanent **"Specific Addiction: Blood (2)"** Character Flaw.

The Dhampir also gains the following bonuses:

- (+40) permanent modifier to **(Esoteric) Mythological: Dhampir**
- (+20) permanent modifier to **(Esoteric) Mythological: Vamps**
- (+20) permanent modifier to **(Survival) Forage: Night Time**
- (+20) permanent modifier to Life Pool
- (+15) permanent modifier to Soul Pool

Notes about the dhampir:

- Silver stops them from healing in any form as long as it is touching their skin. Unlike vampires, silver does not cause extra damage if used in a weapon.
- Sunlight can cause severe sunburn very quickly.
- Lifespan is a typical human lifespan. Dhampir tend to look younger than their actual age until they become addicted to blood. Then they eventually start looking older and more haggard than their actual age.

DHAMPHYR

The Dhamphyr gains three Talents:

Manipulate Aura

- Roll a JDG SC (Target 20). Costs (-5) Soul Pool.
- The dhamphyr can touch their target and manipulate the emotions of their target. The target makes an ALR SC (Target 40) to resist emotional change. If the resist ALR is unsuccessful, the dhamphyr chooses the particular emotional response and the strength of that response.

Aura Empathy

- Roll a JDG SC (Target 10). Costs (-1) Soul Pool.
- The dhamphyr can read the emotions and feelings of their target for up to five minutes. The target must be within visual sight of the dhamphyr, and within a range 3.

Feed the Soul

- When a dhamphyr can physically touch someone with their palm, they can channel their heritage and heal their Soul Pool. When they directly feed, they gain (+20) Soul Pool, while draining (-10) Soul Pool from the target. They can feed once every ten minutes.
- When they feed off the Soul Pool of another being, they risk becoming addicted to the euphoria from the feeding. If they feed too often (too many times per day), the GM may have the dhamphyr make a JDG SC (Target 30). If they fail, they gain a permanent "**Specific Addiction: Emotional Drain (2)**" Character Flaw.

The dhamphyr also gains the following bonuses:

- (+40) permanent modifier to **(Esoteric) Mythological: Dhamphyr**
- (+20) permanent modifier to **(Esoteric) Mythological: Vamps**
- (+20) permanent modifier to **(Influence) Negotiation: Manipulation**
- (+20) permanent modifier to Soul Pool
- (+15) permanent modifier to Life Pool

Notes about the dhamphyr:

- Silver stops them from healing in any form as long as it is touching their skin. Unlike vampires, silver does not cause extra damage if used in a weapon.
- Sunlight can cause severe sunburn very quickly.
- Lifespan is a typical human lifespan. Dhampir tend to look younger than their actual age until they become addicted to emotional feeding. Then they eventually start looking older and more haggard than their actual age.

DEMIGOD

The Demigod gains three Talents and a Curse:

Born of the Pantheon

- Roll a JDG SC (Target 20). Costs (-5) Soul Pool.
- Pick a non-combat Proficiency related to the godly heritage of the character. Once activated the character automatically succeeds on their next attempt to use that Proficiency. The success counts as a Wild Success, allowing for other bonuses during skill use. *For instance, a child of Loki might create an illusionary disguise, or a child of Hermes might know all languages.*

Born of Multiple Worlds

- The character's divine lineage gives them resistance to the environments ruled by their godly heritage. The character gains a (+15) conditional modifier to any **Survival** SC to resist environmental effects that relate to their domain. *For instance, a child of Neptune would gain the modifier for water, the desert for a child of Ra, and so on.* This also applies to traveling to the divine domain of the character's pantheon.

Born with Talent

- Work with your GM to build a talent that further represents your character's godly parentage. For this Talent, use the Faith Ability system in the Refined Core manual to create a faith ability with a maximum SC of (90). Once chosen, instead of the normal Cast SC and Soul pool Drain, the demigod will roll a JDG SC (Target 20) to cast, and drain (-5) Soul Pool when cast. As a Talent, the ability casts in 1 round, regardless of calculated cast time.

Curse of the Pantheon

- Your curse is directly related to your godly parentage. Be it Achilies' heel, Pandora's curiosity, or some other terrible thing you've been cursed with something. *This curse is a Talent controlled by the GM.* This power should be big and important. Like the demigod heroes of old your curse sets you apart from the mortal world making it sometimes difficult to live within the norms of society. *For instance, Imp has a time-traveling curse where he will automatically "bamf" out of time and be transported in time and space to the location where he can retrieve an important artifact. Imp's player has no control over when Imp "bamfs" out – only the GM controls the Talent.*

The demigod also gains the following bonuses:

- (+40) permanent modifier to **(Esoteric) Pantheon: Demigod**
- (+20) permanent modifier to **(Esoteric) Pantheon: [Own Pantheon]**
- (+20) permanent modifier to **[Single Expertise Related to Heritage]**
- (+35) permanent modifier to Life Pool
- (+15) permanent modifier to Soul Pool
- (+15) conditional modifier to all Healing *rolls*, not to the healing results. This applies to healing attempts for both the Life Pool and Soul Pool.

Notes about the demigod:

- Generally live slightly longer than the average human.
- Are usually not fully accepted in their pantheon heritage.

FAELINGS

The Faeling has three Talents and a Curse:

Fae Heritage

- Roll a JDG SC (Target 20). Costs (-5) Soul Pool.
- Pick a non-combat Proficiency related to the fae heritage of the character. Once activated the character automatically succeeds on their next attempt to use that Proficiency. The success counts as a Wild Success, allowing for other bonuses during skill use. *For instance, a druid could make plants grow, a brownie might be able to keep rooms clean, etc.*

Fae Glamor

- The character has the ability to blend into any environment as though they belong there. Their appearance changes in small ways to fit their surroundings. The faeling gains a (+15) conditional modifier to **Survival: Stealth** when wanting to blend into their surroundings.

Fae Talent

- Work with your GM to build a talent that further represents your character's fae heritage. For this Talent, use the Faith Ability system in the Refined Core manual to create a faith ability with a maximum SC of (90). Once chosen, instead of the normal Cast SC and Soul pool Drain, the faeling will roll a JDG SC (Target 20) to cast, and drain (-5) Soul Pool when cast. As a Talent, the ability casts in 1 round, regardless of calculated cast time. *NOTE: Any damage or healing from the ability is calculated with the original SC.*

Fae Curse

- The faeling is connected to the fae realm through their heritage. Because of this, they retain some of the weaknesses of their heritage. Cold Iron interferes with all fae powers, including Talents and faith abilities. Like the fae, the faeling's bargain is their bond. If they willingly enter into a contract with anyone, they must fulfill it as bargained, or the magic of fate itself turns against them. After a betrayal, the fated faeling receives a (-30) conditional modifier to all SC and OC attempts until the bargain is corrected and completed.

The faeling also gains the following bonuses.

- (+40) permanent modifier to **(Esoteric) Fae: Faeling**
- (+20) permanent modifier to **(Esoteric) Fae: [Own Fae-Subtype]**
- (+20) permanent modifier to **[Single Expertise Related to Heritage]**
- (+15) permanent modifier to Life Pool
- (+35) permanent modifier to Soul Pool
- (+15) conditional modifier to all Healing *rolls*, not to the healing results. This applies to healing attempts for both the Life Pool and Soul Pool.

Notes about the faeling:

- Generally live longer than the average human.
- Faelings are generally looked upon as the lowest members of fae society.
- Despite being looked down upon, the faeling will generally need to align themselves with one of the fae courts.

SIMIAN

Simian cryptids have three Talents:

Step Through

- Roll a JDG SC (Target 20). Costs (-5) Soul Pool.
- The simian cryptid is able to step from one major environmental feature to a similar one, based on the type of cryptid. The cryptid is able to Step Through the terrain they are normally found in – sasquatch and skunk apes step through trees, yeti step through piles of snow, and so on. The cryptid can step directly from one environmental feature to another within their line of sight, or they can risk a further step up to a range of (7), however, the cryptid rolls an LCK SC (Target 20) to avoid appearing directly in sight of another being or directly in the path of danger.

Disrupt Surveillance

- Roll a JDG SC (Target 10). Costs (-1) Soul Pool.
- The simian cryptid is naturally capable of disrupting electronic surveillance within a range (5) around them. The nature of their body does not allow them to be photographed easily. The scenery around the cryptid will stay crystal clear, but their body will blur and/or disappear. The simian cryptid must make the JDG SC to turn *off* the ability for up to one hour. The drain only happens when the cryptid turns the Talent off.

Thick Skin

- The simian cryptid skin is thicker than it looks. Their skin provides a natural armor of -/15/15.

The simian cryptid also gains the following bonuses:

- (+40) permanent modifier to **(Esoteric) Cryptid: Simian**
- (+20) permanent modifier to **(Survival) Forage: [Natural Habitat]**
- (+20) permanent modifier to **Survival**
- (+40) points to use on **Survival-based Proficiencies**

Notes about the simian cryptids:

- Sasquatch are usually about Human Average height and longer lived (Max out around 450-500 years). When they die, they go into the tree, and never come out, then the clan has a celebratory wake. Squatch are very communal.
- Yeti are taller, usually at Human Giant height, and usually slightly longer lived than humans (150-200 years). When they die, they disappear into a blizzard/snowstorm. Yeti are loners and only get together to mate.

REPTILIAN

Reptilian cryptids gain three Talents:

Sway the Crowd

- Roll a JDG SC (Target 20). Costs (-5) Soul Pool.
- The reptilian can use their charm and appeal and sway the crowd. The reptilian gains the attention of a crowd within their sight, and can easily sway them toward either benevolence and agreement, or disagreement and targeted anger. This push artificially sways the crowd for ten minutes, after which the reptilian can make an **Influence** SC to maintain their influence.

Alter Perception

- Roll a JDG SC (Target 10). Costs (-1) Soul Pool.
- The reptilian can focus their concentration and change their appearance, re-aligning their glamour to a new look. The changes are minor, and only last ten minutes, but it is usually enough to make them unrecognizable.

Limb Regeneration

- If a full limb is removed, the reptilian will regrow the limb relatively rapidly. It takes about a week to replace an arm, or two weeks to replace a leg, but the limb will eventually grow back, including any then-current scars or other disfigurements.
- If only part of the limb is removed, the growth time is the same.
- Minimum loss of the entire hand or entire foot to affect regrowth.
- Reptilian is far more hungry during the regrowth and risks lethargy or even starvation if not fed more often than normal.

The reptilian cryptid also gains the following bonuses:

- Reptilians have a natural glamour to appear human, although other reptilians can see through the glamour if they choose. They can use the **Alter Perception** Talent to turn off the glamour as well.
- (+40) permanent modifier to **(Esoteric) Cryptid: Reptilian**
- (+10) permanent modifier to **Culture: Assimilation**
- (+10) permanent modifier to **Influence: Deception**

Notes about reptilian cryptids:

- Reptilians live an average human lifespan.
- Reptilians have two rigid castes in their hidden society.

    - Panishti are the elites and upper caste of the reptilians
    - Avar are the lower caste of the reptilians

WINGED

The Winged cryptids gain three Talents:

Wing Fu

- Roll a JDG SC (Target 20). Costs (-5) Soul Pool.
- When the winged cryptid gets into unarmed or melee combat, they can use their wings in combat to confuse and perplex their opponent. When active, Wing Fu lasts for ten rounds. When they activate Wing Fu, any time they successfully defend against an unarmed or melee attack they can immediately make a counterattack (a riposte).
- The cryptid's prior defense OC becomes their attack OC, and the original attacker must make an appropriate defensive OC. Normal damages apply.

One with the Night

- Roll a JDG SC (Target 10). Costs (-1) Soul Pool.
- The winged cryptid can blend into any shadow or darkness for up to 10 minutes, as long as it is sized to fit them.
- Requires a Survival: Awareness SC (Target 120) by the observer to detect the cryptid.

Falling with Style

- When a winged cryptid is at a height of at least 4, it can glide to land safely. From a height of 4 or 5, the cryptid makes an HEC SC (Target 20) to land successfully. From a height of 6, the cryptid makes an HEC SC (Target 25) to land successfully. From a height of 7, the cryptid makes an HEC SC (Target 30) to land successfully. From a height of 8 or more, the cryptid must make an HEC SC (Target 50) to land successfully. Where and how far away the cryptid lands are determined by the successes of the HEC and the GM.

The winged cryptid also gains the following bonuses:

- (+40) permanent modifier to **(Esoteric) Cryptid: Winged**
- (+15) permanent modifier to **Survival: Awareness**
- (+15) permanent modifier to **Combat**
- (+40) points to use on **Combat-based Proficiencies** (excluding Ranged and Explosives)

Notes about winged cryptids:

- Moth-folk and bird-folk are solitary beings, other than brooding mothers, and are VERY rare.
- Moth-folk and bird-folk have slightly shorter lifespans than the average human. They are about as tall as the average human.
- Gargoyles are communal beings, living in clans based on the building they are protecting.
- Gargoyles are very short, averaging about human dwarf height, and have slightly shorter lifespans than the average human.
- All winged cryptids can stay motionless for long periods of time, usually unaffected by weather.

CANID

The Canid cryptids gain three Talents:

Bloodhound

- Roll a JDG SC (Target 20). Costs (-5) Soul Pool.
- The canid cryptid can use their Bloodhound Talent to track a single being for six hours, regardless of where they go and what tricks they use. The canid will know the direction and be able to follow the trail, even if they get in a vehicle. *Note: This cannot track across different realm barriers.*

Howl at the Moon

- Roll a JDG SC (Target 10). Costs (-1) Soul Pool.
- The canid can communicate over long distances with howls and sounds, up to a range of 9. They can connect with any canid cryptid within range, communicating complex ideas and receiving answers.

Pack Attack

- Canids work in packs. The canid cryptid gains a (+5) conditional modifier for any action taken in coordination with another pack member. This includes combat actions. *GM Discretion Applies.*

The canid cryptid also gains the following bonuses:

- (+40) permanent modifier to **(Esoteric) Cryptid: Canid**
- (+25) conditional modifier to **Combat: Unarmed** for Grapple/Hold actions.
- (+20) permanent modifier to **Survival**
- (+40) points to use on **Survival-based Proficiencies**

Notes about canid cryptids:

- Canids are pack animals, and do not feel secure when outside their pack (either canid pack or adopted team pack).
- Canids hate being in the limelight, and generally prefer to be unnoticed in society.

CONSTRUCTS

Constructs gain three Talents and one Fatal Flaw:

Hot Swap

- Roll a JDG SC (Target 20). Costs (-5) Soul Pool.
- The construct can attach a replacement limb/body part where there is one missing. This requires the appropriate raw materials or body parts. The new part fuses with the body and becomes part of the body. The healing is automatic and does not require a Healing roll for their Life Pool.
- The GM determines if the construct has gathered sufficient raw materials. If they have not, the GM will help determine how many Life Pool points the character regains.

Reconstruct Self

- Roll a JDG SC (Target 17). Costs (-3) Soul Pool.
- The construct can temporarily restructure its physical attributes directly for a total of ten minutes, disregarding any normal limits. The physical attributes are: MIG, HEA, HEC, and QCK. The construct can do this (JDG/5) times per day. *For instance, if the construct has a MIG of (21) and an HEC of (12), the construct can swap those two numbers, even though the construct would normally have a maximum of (13) for HEC. In this case, the construct would have a MIG of (12), but an HEC of (21) for those ten minutes.*

Just a Scratch

- Roll a JDG SC (Target 10). Costs (-1) Soul Pool.
- The construct can force a completely damaged limb or body part to continue to work even if damaged for ten minutes. Damaged limbs will work at normal capacity until the Talent expires.

Fatal Flaw

- Every construct has a Spark of Life that is in a special part of their head. If the head or the container for the Spark of Life is destroyed, the construct dies.
- Flesh constructs carry their Spark of Life in their skull, sometimes protected inside a specially prepared box.
- Clockwork constructs carry their Spark of Life in a Harmonic Oscillator that is carried in their head.
- Sculpted constructs carry their Spark of Life in a *keley emett* inside their head.

The construct also gains the following bonuses:

Flesh Construct

- (+20) permanent modifier to **Survival**
- (+60) points to use for **Survival-based Proficiencies**

Clockwork Constructs

- (+20) permanent modifier to **Handicraft**
- (+60) points to use for **Handicraft-based Proficiencies**

Sculpted Constructs

- (+20) permanent modifier to **System**
- (+60) points to use for **System-based Proficiencies**

All Constructs

- (+25) to Life Pool

Notes about constructs:

- Constructs feel no pain, therefore any Combat Modifiers based on pain do not apply.
- Constructs cannot heal Life Pool by any means other than the **Hot Swap** Talent. The construct must have the appropriate materials in order to replace/repair their damaged parts. Constructs heal Soul Pool normally.

THE CHANGED OTHER
CHAPTER THREE

Building a Changed Other character is different from building a Created Other. Created Others have their own version of character creation. On the other hand, Changed Others are human characters who have been converted, or changed, into an Other. Building a Changed Other character is a two-step process. The first step is to go through basic Character Creation from the Refined Core handbook. Then the character is modified into a Changed Other.

This chapter can also be used in gameplay if a character is infected or afflicted and converted into a Changed Other. If the conversion happens during gameplay, skip Step 1 and find the correct Other for your character's conversion. Follow the steps there.

STEP 1 – BASIC CHARACTER CREATION

The first step is to build a character in Character Creation in the *Hidden Worlds Refined Core* handbook. Go through every step in the process except for Step 2 (Aspect Chart) and Step 11 (The Incursion Event). In this case, your character's incursion event is them becoming a Changed Other.

STEP 2 – CHANGED OTHERS

At this step, choose your Changed Other, and work with the GM to figure out how long your character has been that Changed Other. This time may change your character's age, or you can incorporate the change into the current age of your character. *NOTE: If you add age/years to your character, you will need to determine what your character has done for those intervening years, including any additional years in their career. Any additional years in the career should be reflected in the skills.*

If your character is changed during gameplay, the character starts at the initial age stage for the Changed Other, if it has any.

In both instances, refer to the appropriate Other description for the changes that happen to your character. For a Changed Other, it is recommended that the player rewrites their new character on one of the Other character sheets, instead of trying to erase and fill in their current character sheet.

VAMPIRE

Vampires are humans with a virus born from the nightmare realm. Unless they are in the Undead stage, the vampire can appear as a mostly normal human being, unless their monster is unleashed. When the monster is unleashed, they physically change. There are three playable age stages for vampires, based on their state of life, and how often they have fed.

Summary

The Monster: The monster side of the vampire has black orbs for eyes flecked with motes of glowing red. All of their teeth sharpen into points, not just the canines. Fingernails and toenails lengthen, thicken, and sharpen, creating claws. Blood/color drains from the skin, and they get very pale.

Feeding: Vampires generally feed by ripping open the skin and veins to drain the blood from a living being. They need fresh, or fairly fresh, blood to live. Feeding is usually messy and leaves scars and gaping wounds. When a vampire bites a living being, their teeth release a numbing agent. After a few seconds, the pain is lessened and pleasure is derived from the contact. Once the numbing agent starts working, the victim has a slim chance of breaking free from the hold (JDG SC, Target 30).

Living victims of vampires are typically woozy and feel their energy drained. Any normal actions by the victim receive a (-15) conditional modifier for ten minutes after the vampire has fed. Also, the victim generally has a bleeding wound that needs to be medically treated before the blood loss becomes dangerous.

When a vampire feeds on another vampire, vampyre, dhampir, or dhamphyr, they get violently ill and gain the **Major Distraction** condition for one minute.

When a vampire feeds directly on a fae taking at least one unit of blood, they get euphoric and gain a (+20) conditional modifier to all rolls for ten rounds.

It is possible for vampires to maintain/sustain their unlife/undeath with relatively fresh blood that has been harvested elsewhere. This blood must remain "unspoiled" and must be relatively fresh.

NOTE: Only unspoiled blood will restore the Life Pool of a vampire, and only fresh blood from a living creature will restore the Soul Pool of a vampire.

Unlife vs. Undeath: A living Vampire is considered to have "Unlife", and can usually maintain their relatively human experience. Under stress, or at will, the vampire can change. Their eyes become solid black orbs (giving them black and white low-light vision), their claws grow out from their fingers, and their teeth become pointed (all of them).

If they are turned at the point of death, or if they are "nearly killed" to (0) Soul Pool while a Living Vampire, they become "Undead." An Undead Vampire can no longer hide their monster.

Age and Appearance: After infection, vampires age about one year for every ten years that humans age.

Permanent Death: To kill a vampire, the vampire's head must be destroyed or removed, or it must be damaged enough to go to (-10) Life Pool *and* (-10) Soul Pool.

Age Stages

There are three playable age stages for the vampire: Immature, Living, and Undead.

IMMATURE VAMPIRE

Immature vampires are those that have just turned, and still have an unstable connection to the nightmare *Coşmar* realm. This is the one stage where the character can be cured of their vampire infection. The immature stage lasts until the vampire feeds on their first living blood.

To cure an immature vampire, the link to the nightmare realm must be broken by killing the vampire sire/dam and then killing the virus, before the vampire feeds on blood from a living being. To kill the virus (after killing the sire/dam), the vampire must be subjected to a Faith Ability designed to further sever the connection to that realm. If both killing the sire/dam and the Faith Ability is completed before the immature vampire feeds on fresh blood, the curse is broken, and the human retains no remnants of the vampire curse.

The immature vampire cannot spread the virus to any other victim, except an unborn baby, as in the case of the birth of a Dhampir.

Immature vampires change the JDG Attribute. In the chart below, refer to the character's current JDG and change it to the New JDG.

JDG	
Current	New
1	1
2	1
3	2
4	2
5	3
6	3
7	4
8	4
9	5
10	5
11	6
12	6
13	7
14	7
15	8
16	9
17	10
18	11
19	12
20	13

The immature vampire gains the following Talent:

Regeneration

- If a vampire takes damage to their Life Pool, the vampire starts to immediately draw from their Soul Pool on a 1:1 basis to regenerate their Life Pool and heal the damage.
- The vampire gains (+2) Life Pool/round, with a corresponding (-2) Soul Pool/round drain.
- The Regeneration occurs until the damage is healed or until the vampire reaches (0) Soul Pool.
- The vampire can choose to turn off the Regeneration by making a JDG SC (Target 15).

The immature vampire also gains the following bonuses:

Vampire Healing

- When the character feeds, they make a HEA healing roll, and it applies to **both** Life Pool and Soul Pool.
- To heal Life Pool: the character gains (+2) per unit of food/blood to the RESULTS of the healing roll.
- To heal Soul Pool: the character gains (+5) per unit of fresh living blood to the RESULTS of the healing roll.
- *For instance, if the character consumed three units of living blood from a victim to feed, they would make a HEA-based healing roll, and apply the results to both the Life Pool and Soul Pool, with the following modifiers: (+6) to Life Pool and (+15) to Soul Pool.*

Sharpened Senses

- The character gains a (+10) permanent modifier to **Survival: Awareness**
- Low Light Vision - the character can see in low light situations, although their low-light vision is in black and white, without color distinction.

Vitality in Death

- (+20) Life Pool
- (+10) Soul Pool

The immature vampire also gains the following weaknesses:

Bloodlust

- If an immature vampire takes any Life Pool damage, they must make a JDG SC (Target 20) to avoid entering bloodlust.
- If they fail the roll, they will immediately attack anyone around them to feed, starting with wounded beings. The bloodlust vampire must make another JDG SC (Target 25) to avoid attacking friends, allies, and team members.

Photosensitivity

- The character takes (-3) Life Pool damage *per minute* when exposed to direct sunlight or strong UV light. Covering exposed skin negates this damage.

Silver

- Vampires react negatively to silver, as it is considered a "pure" metal.
- Direct silver contact on the body will negate the Regeneration Talent.
- Silver weapons add (+15) total damage to any attack on the vampire.

Wood

- Wood that is lodged in the heart will negate the Regeneration Talent.
- Wood that is lodged through the heart and into the earth will cause complete paralysis of the vampire, and negate the Regeneration Talent.

Unaware while feeding

- When an immature vampire feeds, they become completely unaware of their surroundings.

Faith Symbols

- If the wearer has sincere faith in a faith symbol, that faith symbol will repel or injure a vampire.
- Vampire receives a (-15) conditional modifier to approach or attack a faith symbol bearer.
- Vampire is burned when touched by an active faith symbol and takes (-15) Life Pool damage from each contact.
- *Examples include: A cross for a Christian, a star of David for an orthodox Jew, a pentacle for a Wiccan, or even a compass for a Mason.*

LIVING VAMPIRE

Living vampires are no longer immature and have fed at least once from a living being. They have fully embraced the nightmare realm of *Coșmar*, and have become a creature of the night. A living vampire will stay a living vampire until they get to (0) Soul Pool. A living vampire cannot become a Master vampire.

Living vampires make the following changes to their Attributes. Compare your character's current attribute on the left-hand column, and find the new one under the appropriate column. *Note: If the vampire is changing from Immature to Living, their JDG does not change, because it has already been adjusted.* Use the chart below:

Curr	MIG	QCK	JDG	ALR	Curr	MIG	QCK	JDG	ALR
1	8	8	1	1	11	16	16	6	4
2	8	8	1	1	12	17	17	6	4
3	8	8	2	1	13	18	18	7	5
4	9	9	2	2	14	19	19	7	5
5	9	9	3	2	15	20	20	8	5
6	10	10	3	3	16	20	20	9	6
7	11	11	4	3	17	21	21	10	6
8	12	12	4	3	18	22	22	11	7
9	13	13	5	4	19	23	23	12	7
10	15	15	5	4	20	25	25	13	8

The living vampire gains the following Talents:

Regeneration

- If a vampire takes damage to their Life Pool, the vampire starts to immediately draw from their Soul Pool on a 5:3 basis to regenerate their Life Pool and heal the damage.
- The vampire gains (+5) Life Pool/round, with a corresponding (-3) Soul Pool/round drain.
- The Regeneration occurs until the damage is healed or until the vampire reaches (0) Soul Pool.
- The vampire can choose to turn off the Regeneration by making a JDG SC (Target 15).

Claws and Teeth

- When the character's monster is active, they grow claws and teeth.
- The character gains a (+15) total damage modifier to a bite attack.
- The character Base Strike damage from their claw attacks is changed to 2(+10).

Mind Control

- Can control (JDG/3) victims at a time, and the victims must be within visual range (4) when they become controlled.
- Roll JDG SC (Target 15). Costs (-3) Soul Pool. Roll for each target.
- Control lasts for 1 minute (Success +1 to +5), one hour (Success +6 to +15), or one week (Success +16 or more).
- Control cannot make the victims physically harm themselves, directly harm others, or submit themselves to physical harm from others (except for personal feeding of the vampire).

The living vampire also gains the following bonuses:

Controlling The Monster

- The living vampire can usually control their monster. If the character is under stress or taking damage, the monster wants to come out. The character can accept the monster, or roll a JDG SC (Target 15) to keep it hidden.

Vampire Healing

- When the character feeds, they make a HEA healing roll, and it applies to **both** Life Pool and Soul Pool.
- To heal Life Pool: the character gains (+4) per unit of food/blood to the RESULTS of the healing roll.
- To heal Soul Pool: the character gains (+7) per unit of fresh living blood to the RESULTS of the healing roll.
- *For instance, if the character consumed three units of living blood from a victim to feed, they would make a HEA-based healing roll, and apply the results to both the Life Pool and Soul Pool, with the following modifiers: (+12) to Life Pool and (+21) to Soul Pool.*

Sharpened Senses

- The character gains a (+20) permanent modifier to **Survival: Awareness** - only a (+10) permanent modifier if the character is moving from Immature to a Living vampire.
- Low Light Vision - the character can see in low light situations, although their low-light vision is in black and white, without color distinction.

Naturally Skilled
- Character gains (+20) permanent modifier to **Combat: Unarmed** and **(Combat) Melee: Claws and Teeth**.
- Character gains (+40) permanent modifier to **(Esoteric) Mythological: Vamps**.

Infect Victim
- The bite of a living vampire can infect other humans.
- If a living vampire feeds from a victim, the victim has a low chance of becoming a new vampire. The victim makes an LCK SC (Target 1). If the victim fails, they become an immature vampire.

Vitality in Death
- (+40) Life Pool [only gain (+20) Life Pool if moving from Immature to Living vampire]
- (+20) Soul Pool [only gain (+10) Soul Pool if moving from Immature to Living vampire]

The living vampire also gains the following weaknesses:

Bloodlust
- If a living vampire takes (-10) Life Pool damage in a single round, they must make a JDG SC (Target 20) to avoid entering bloodlust.
- If they fail the roll, they will immediately attack anyone around them to feed, starting with wounded beings. The bloodlust vampire must make another JDG SC (Target 25) to avoid attacking friends, allies, and team members.

Photosensitivity
- The character takes (-5) Life Pool damage *per minute* when exposed to direct sunlight or strong UV light. Covering exposed skin negates this damage.
- When their monster is active, the character takes (-15) Life Pool damage per minute when exposed to sunlight or UV rays.

Silver
- Vampires react negatively to silver, as it is considered a "pure" metal.
- Direct silver contact on the body will negate the Regeneration Talent.
- Silver weapons add 2(+10) total damage to any attack on the vampire.

Wood
- Wood that is lodged in the heart will negate the Regeneration Talent.
- Wood that is lodged through the heart and into the earth will cause complete paralysis to the vampire, and negate the Regeneration Talent.

Unaware while feeding
- When a living vampire feeds, they become completely unaware of their surroundings.

Faith Symbols
- If the wearer has sincere faith in a faith symbol, that faith symbol will repel or injure a vampire.
- Vampire receives a (-20) conditional modifier to approach or attack a faith symbol bearer.
- Vampire is burned when touched by an active faith symbol and takes (-20) Life Pool damage from each contact.
- *Examples include: A cross for a Christian, a star of David for an orthodox Jew, a pentacle for a Wiccan, or even a compass for a Mason.*

UNDEAD VAMPIRE

Undead vampires have passed beyond unlife and have fully embraced their monster. Their connection to the nightmare realm is overwhelming. As an undead vampire, their monster is always evident, and they cannot appear fully human.

Undead vampires make the following changes to their Attributes. Compare your character's current attribute on the left-hand column, and find the new one under the appropriate column. *Note: If the vampire is changing from Living to Undead, their MIG, QCK, JDG, and ALR do not change, because they have already been adjusted.* Use the chart below:

Current	New MIG	New HEA	New QCK	New JDG	New ALR	New HEC
1	8	8	8	1	1	1
2	8	8	8	1	1	1
3	8	8	8	2	1	2
4	9	9	9	2	2	2
5	9	9	9	3	2	3
6	10	10	10	3	3	3
7	11	11	11	4	3	4
8	12	12	12	4	3	4
9	13	13	13	5	4	5
10	15	15	15	5	4	5
11	16	16	16	6	4	6
12	17	17	17	6	4	6
13	18	18	18	7	5	7
14	19	19	19	7	5	7
15	20	20	20	8	5	8
16	20	20	20	9	6	9
17	21	21	21	10	6	10
18	22	22	22	11	7	11
19	23	23	23	12	7	12
20	25	25	25	13	8	13

The undead vampire gains the following Talents:

Regeneration
- If a vampire takes damage to their Life Pool, the vampire starts to immediately draw from their Soul Pool on a 7:2 basis to regenerate their Life Pool and heal the damage.
- The vampire gains (+7) Life Pool/round, with a corresponding (-2) Soul Pool/round drain.
- The Regeneration occurs until the damage is healed or until the vampire reaches (0) Soul Pool.
- The vampire can choose to turn off the Regeneration by making a JDG SC (Target 15).

Claws and Teeth

- When the character's monster is active, they grow claws and teeth.
- The character gains a (+15) total damage modifier to a bite attack.
- The character Base Strike damage from their claw attacks is changed to 2(+10).

Mind Control

- Can control (JDG) victims at a time, and the victims must be within visual range (5) when they become controlled.
- Roll JDG SC (Target 15). Costs (-3) Soul Pool. Roll for each target.
- Control lasts for 1 minute (Success +1 to +5), one hour (Success +6 to +15), or one week (Success +16 or more).
- Control cannot make the victims physically harm themselves, directly harm others, or submit themselves to physical harm from others (except for personal feeding of the vampire).

Create Thrall

- Can create permanent thrall who is their follower/slave. A thrall is created from a victim who is currently under the Mind Control effect from the vampire.
- Roll JDG SC (Target 20). Costs (-5) Soul Pool.
- If the attempt succeeds, the victim makes a JDG OC save, versus the original Thrall roll. If the victim fails, they become a permanent thrall of the undead vampire.

The undead vampire also gains the following bonuses:

Vampire Healing

- When the character feeds, they make a HEA healing roll, and it applies to **both** Life Pool and Soul Pool.
- To heal Life Pool: the character gains (+5) per unit of food/blood to the RESULTS of the healing roll.
- To heal Soul Pool: the character gains (+10) per unit of fresh living blood to the RESULTS of the healing roll.
- *For instance, if the character consumed three units of living blood from a victim to feed, they would make a HEA-based healing roll, and apply the results to both the Life Pool and Soul Pool, with the following modifiers: (+15) to Life Pool and (+30) to Soul Pool.*

Sharpened Senses

- The character gains a (+30) permanent modifier to **Survival: Awareness** - only a (+10) permanent modifier if the character is moving from Living to Undead vampire.
- Low Light Vision - the character can see in low light situations, although their low-light vision is in black and white, without color distinction.

Naturally Skilled (does not apply to the character moving from Living to Undead vampire)

- Character gains (+20) permanent modifier to **Combat: Unarmed** and **(Combat) Melee: Claws and Teeth.**
- Character gains (+40) permanent modifier to **(Esoteric) Mythological: Vamps.**

Infect Victim

- The bite of an undead vampire can infect other humans.
- If an undead vampire feeds from a victim, the victim has a low chance of becoming a new vampire. The victim makes an LCK SC (Target 5). If the victim fails, they become an immature vampire.
- If an undead vampire *chooses* to infect one of their victims, they must roll a JDG SC (Target 20). Costs (-5) Soul Pool. If successful, the victim makes an LCK SC (Target 20) to avoid infection.

Vitality in Death

- (+60) Life Pool [only gain (+20) Life Pool if moving from Living to Undead vampire]
- (+30) Soul Pool [only gain (+10) Soul Pool if moving from Living to Undead vampire]

The undead vampire also gains the following weaknesses:

Bloodlust

- If an undead vampire takes any Life Pool damage, they must make a JDG SC (Target 20) to avoid entering bloodlust.
- If they fail the roll, they will immediately attack anyone around them to feed, starting with wounded beings. The bloodlust vampire must make another JDG SC (Target 25) to avoid attacking friends, allies, and team members.

Photosensitivity

- The character takes (-30) Life Pool damage *per round* when exposed to direct sunlight or strong UV light.
- The character takes (-10) Life Pool damage *per round* when exposed to any sunlight or UV rays.

Silver

- Vampires react negatively to silver, as it is considered a "pure" metal.
- Direct silver contact on the body will negate the Regeneration Talent.
- Silver weapons add 3(+10) total damage to any attack on the vampire.

Wood

- Wood that is lodged in the heart will negate the Regeneration Talent.
- Wood that is lodged through the heart and into the earth will cause complete paralysis to the vampire, and negate the Regeneration Talent.

Unaware while feeding

- When an undead vampire feeds, they become completely unaware of their surroundings.

Faith Symbols

- If the wearer has sincere faith in a faith symbol, that faith symbol will repel or injure a vampire.
- Vampire receives a (-30) conditional modifier to approach or attack a faith symbol bearer.
- Vampire is burned when touched by an active faith symbol and takes (-30) Life Pool damage from each contact.
- *Examples include: A cross for a Christian, a star of David for an orthodox Jew, a pentacle for a Wiccan, or even a compass for a Mason.*

VAMPYRE

A vampyre's monster is not scary but it is terrifying to those that have seen it and lived to tell the tale. Their features become uncannily perfect. No imperfection touches their bodies. Those that escape have stories of white eyes that went on forever. There are three playable age stages for vampires, based on their state of life, and how often they have fed.

Summary

The Monster: The monster side of the vampire has white orbs for eyes flecked with motes of glowing red. Blood/color drains from the skin, and they get very pale.

Feeding: A vampyre feed from the victim's Soul Pool, either through indirect feed or directly through touch. Feeding for a vampyre requires skin-to-skin contact, with their hand or mouth on the victim's skin, with the best position being over the victim's heart. When the hand is used for feeding, a lamprey-like mouth appears in the palm to make the connection. It takes a few seconds to make the connection to start feeding. Once feeding has begun, the victim will enter a euphoric state (JDG SC, Target 30 to break).

When a vampyre feeds directly on another vampyre, vampire, dhamphyr, or dhampir, they get violently ill and gain the **Major Distraction** condition for one minute.

When a vampyre feeds directly on a fae taking at least one Soul Pool, they get euphoric and gain a (+20) conditional modifier to all rolls for ten rounds.

It is possible for vampyres to maintain/sustain their unlife/undeath by harvesting from environmental emotions.

NOTE: While indirect emotional feeding will restore the Life Pool of a vampyre, only direct feeding from a living creature will restore the Soul Pool of a vampyre.

Unlife vs. Undeath: A living Vampyre is considered to have "Unlife", and can usually maintain their relatively human experience. Under stress, or at will, the vampire can change. Their eyes become solid white orbs (giving them black and white low-light vision).

If they are turned at the point of death, or if they are "nearly killed" to (0) Soul Pool while a Living Vampyre, they become "Undead." An Undead Vampyre can only hide their monster with their glamour.

Age and Appearance: After infection, vampyres age about one year for every ten years that humans age.

Permanent Death: To kill a vampyre, the vampyre's head must be destroyed or removed, or they must be damaged enough to go to (-10) Life Pool *and* (-10) Soul Pool.

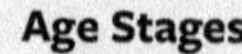

There are three playable age stages for the vampyre: Immature, Living, and Undead.

IMMATURE VAMPYRE

Immature vampyres are those that have just turned, and still have an unstable connection to the nightmare *Coşmar* realm. This is the one stage where the character can be cured of their vampyre infection. The immature stage lasts until the vampyre feeds on their first living blood.

To cure an immature vampyre, the link to the nightmare realm must be broken by killing the vampyre sire/dam and then killing the virus, before the vampyre feeds directly from a living being. To kill the virus (after killing the sire/dam), the vampyre must be subjected to a Faith Ability designed to further sever the connection to that realm. If both killing the sire/dam and the Faith Ability is completed before the immature vampyre feeds directly from a living being, the curse is broken, and the human retains no remnants of the vampyre curse.

The immature vampyre cannot spread the virus to any other victim, except an unborn baby, as in the case of the birth of a Dhamphyr.

Immature vampyres change the JDG Attribute. In the chart below, refer to the character's current JDG and change it to the New JDG.

JDG	
Current	New
1	1
2	1
3	2
4	2
5	3
6	3
7	4
8	4
9	5
10	5
11	6
12	6
13	7
14	7
15	8
16	9
17	10
18	11
19	12
20	13

The immature vampyre gains the following Talent:

Regeneration

- If a vampyre takes damage to their Life Pool, the vampyre starts to immediately draw from their Soul Pool on a 1:1 basis to regenerate their Soul Pool and heal the damage.
- The vampyre gains (+2) Life Pool/round, with a corresponding (-2) Soul Pool/round drain.
- The Regeneration occurs until the damage is healed or until the vampyre reaches (0) Soul Pool.
- The vampyre can choose to turn off the Regeneration by making a JDG SC (Target 20).

The immature vampyre also gains the following bonuses:

Vampyre Healing
- When the character feeds, they make a JDG healing roll, and it applies to **both** Life Pool and Soul Pool.
- To heal Life Pool: the character gains (+2) to the RESULTS of the healing roll per Soul Pool they drain from the victim.
- To heal Soul Pool: the character gains (+5) to the RESULTS of the healing roll per Soul Pool they directly drain from the victim.
- *For instance, if the character consumed three Soul Pool points directly from a victim to feed, they would make a JDG-based healing roll, and apply the results to both the Life Pool and Soul Pool, with the following modifiers: (+6) to Life Pool and (+15) to Soul Pool.*

Beautiful Beast
- The character gains a (+10) permanent modifier to **Influence: Deception**.

Vitality in Death
- (+10) Life Pool
- (+20) Soul Pool

The immature vampyre also gains the following weaknesses:

Soulfrenzy
- If an immature vampyre takes any Life Pool damage, they must make a JDG SC (Target 20) to avoid entering soulfrenzy.
- If they fail the roll, they will immediately attack anyone around them to feed, starting with wounded beings. The soulfrenzy vampire must make another JDG SC (Target 25) to avoid attacking friends, allies, and team members.

Photosensitivity
- The character takes (-3) Life Pool damage *per minute* when exposed to direct sunlight or strong UV light. Covering exposed skin negates this damage.

Silver
- Vampyres react negatively to silver, as it is considered a "pure" metal.
- Direct silver contact on the body will negate the Regeneration Talent.
- Silver weapons add (+15) total damage to any attack on the vampyre.

Wood
- Wood that is lodged in the heart will negate the Regeneration Talent.
- Wood that is lodged through the heart and into the earth will cause complete paralysis to the vampyre, and negate the Regeneration Talent.

Unaware while feeding
- When an immature vampyre feeds, they become completely unaware of their surroundings.

Faith Symbols
- If the wearer has sincere faith in a faith symbol, that faith symbol will repel or injure a vampire.
- Vampyre receives a (-15) conditional modifier to approach or attack a faith symbol bearer.
- Vampyre is burned when touched by an active faith symbol and takes (-15) Life Pool damage from each contact.
- *Examples include: A cross for a Christian, a star of David for an orthodox Jew, a pentacle for a Wiccan, or even a compass for a Mason.*

LIVING VAMPYRE

Living vampyres are no longer immature and have fed at least once from a living being. They have fully embraced the nightmare realm of *Coşmar*, and have become a creature of the night. A living vampyre will stay a living vampyre until they get to (0) Soul Pool. A living vampyre cannot become a Master vampire.

Living vampyres make the following changes to their Attributes. Compare your character's current attribute on the left-hand column, and find the new one under the appropriate column. *Note: If the vampyre is changing from Immature to Living, their MIG does not change, because it has already been adjusted.* Use the chart below:

Curr	ALR	HEC	JDG	MIG	Curr	ALR	HEC	JDG	MIG
1	8	8	1	1	11	16	16	6	4
2	8	8	1	1	12	17	17	6	4
3	8	8	2	1	13	18	18	7	5
4	9	9	2	2	14	19	19	7	5
5	9	9	3	2	15	20	20	8	5
6	10	10	3	3	16	20	20	9	6
7	11	11	4	3	17	21	21	10	6
8	12	12	4	3	18	22	22	11	7
9	13	13	5	4	19	23	23	12	7
10	15	15	5	4	20	25	25	13	8

The living vampyre gains the following Talents:

Regeneration

- If a vampyre takes damage to their Life Pool, the vampire starts to immediately draw from their Soul Pool on a 5:3 basis to regenerate their Life Pool and heal the damage.
- The vampyre gains (+5) Life Pool/round, with a corresponding (-3) Soul Pool/round drain.
- The Regeneration occurs until the damage is healed or until the vampyre reaches (0) Soul Pool.
- The vampyre can choose to turn off the Regeneration by making a JDG SC (Target 15).

Overwhelming Aura

- The vampyre can choose to overwhelm the aura of a victim and paralyze them into inaction. The vampyre must be in direct contact with the victim.
- Roll JDG SC (Target 15). Costs (-3) Soul Pool.
- Paralysis lasts for one minute (Success +1 to +5), ten minutes (Success +6 to +15), or one hour (Success +16 or more).

Feed from the Crowd

- When surrounded by a crowd with high emotions, the vampyre can feed indirectly.
- Roll JDG SC (Target 10). Costs (-1) Soul Pool.
- Vampyre draws (1) Soul Pool per minute from the crowd. This energy can be used to heal the life pool (per Vampyre Healing), but not the Soul Pool.

The living vampyre also gains the following bonuses:

Controlling The Monster

- The living vampyre can usually control their monster. If the character is under stress or taking damage, the monster wants to come out. The character can accept the monster, or roll a JDG SC (Target 15) to keep it hidden.

Vampyre Healing

- When the character feeds, they make a JDG healing roll, and it applies to **both** Life Pool and Soul Pool.
- To heal Life Pool: the character gains (+4) to the RESULTS of the healing roll per Soul Pool Drained.
- To heal Soul Pool: the character gains (+7) to the RESULTS of the healing roll, per Soul Pool drained.
- *For instance, if the character consumed three Soul Pool from a victim to feed, they would make a JDG-based healing roll, and apply the results to both the Life Pool and Soul Pool, with the following modifiers: (+12) to Life Pool and (+21) to Soul Pool.*

Beautiful Beast

- The character gains a (+20) permanent modifier to **Influence: Deception**. *NOTE: if the character is moving from Immature to Living vampyre, the character only gains (+10) to Influence: Deception.*

Naturally Skilled

- Character gains (+20) permanent modifier to **Influence: Negotiation** and **(Survival) Stealth: Crowds**.
- Character gains (+40) permanent modifier to **(Esoteric) Mythological: Vamps**.

Infect Victim

- The direct feeding of a living vampyre can infect other humans.
- If a living vampyre directly feeds from a victim, the victim has a low chance of becoming a new vampyre. The victim makes an LCK SC (Target 1). If the victim fails, they become an immature vampyre.

Vitality in Death

- (+20) Life Pool [only gain (+10) Life Pool if moving from Immature to Living vampyre]
- (+40) Soul Pool [only gain (+20) Soul Pool if moving from Immature to Living vampyre]

The living vampire also gains the following weaknesses:

Soulfrenzy

- If a living vampyre takes (-10) Life Pool damage in a single round, they must make a JDG SC (Target 20) to avoid entering soulfrenzy.
- If they fail the roll, they will immediately attack anyone around them to feed, starting with wounded beings. The soulfrenzy vampyre must make another JDG SC (Target 25) to avoid attacking friends, allies, and team members.

Photosensitivity

- The character takes (-5) Life Pool damage *per minute* when exposed to direct sunlight or strong UV light. Covering exposed skin negates this damage.
- When their monster is active, the character takes (-15) Life Pool damage per minute when exposed to sunlight or UV rays.

Silver

- Vampyres react negatively to silver, as it is considered a "pure" metal.
- Direct silver contact on the body will negate the Regeneration Talent.
- Silver weapons add 2(+10) total damage to any attack on the vampire.

Wood

- Wood that is lodged in the heart will negate the Regeneration Talent.
- Wood that is lodged through the heart and into the earth will cause complete paralysis to the vampyre, and negate the Regeneration Talent.

Unaware while feeding

- When a living vampyre feeds, they become completely unaware of their surroundings.

Faith Symbols

- If the wearer has sincere faith in a faith symbol, that faith symbol will repel or injure a vampyre.
- Vampyre receives a (-20) conditional modifier to approach or attack a faith symbol bearer.
- Vampyre is burned when touched by an active faith symbol and takes (-20) Life Pool damage from each contact.
- *Examples include: A cross for a Christian, a star of David for an orthodox Jew, a pentacle for a Wiccan, or even a compass for a Mason.*

UNDEAD VAMPYRE

Undead vampyres have passed beyond unlife and have fully embraced their monster. Their connection to the nightmare realm is overwhelming. As an undead vampire, their beautiful monster is always evident, and they cannot appear fully human.

Undead vampyres make the following changes to their Attributes. Compare your character's current attribute on the left-hand column, and find the new one under the appropriate column. *Note: If the vampyre is changing from Living to Undead, their ALR, HEC, JDG, and MIG do not change, because they have already been adjusted.* Use the chart below:

Current	New MIG	New HEA	New QCK	New JDG	New ALR	New HEC
1	8	8	8	1	1	1
2	8	8	8	1	1	1
3	8	8	8	2	1	2
4	9	9	9	2	2	2
5	9	9	9	3	2	3
6	10	10	10	3	3	3
7	11	11	11	4	3	4
8	12	12	12	4	3	4
9	13	13	13	5	4	5
10	15	15	15	5	4	5
11	16	16	16	6	4	6
12	17	17	17	6	4	6
13	18	18	18	7	5	7
14	19	19	19	7	5	7
15	20	20	20	8	5	8
16	20	20	20	9	6	9
17	21	21	21	10	6	10
18	22	22	22	11	7	11
19	23	23	23	12	7	12
20	25	25	25	13	8	13

The undead vampyre gains the following Talents:

Regeneration

- If a vampyre takes damage to their Life Pool, the vampyre starts to immediately draw from their Soul Pool on a 7:2 basis to regenerate their Life Pool and heal the damage.
- The vampyre gains (+7) Life Pool/round, with a corresponding (-2) Soul Pool/round drain.
- The Regeneration occurs until the damage is healed or until the vampyre reaches (0) Soul Pool.
- The vampyre can choose to turn off the Regeneration by making a JDG SC (Target 15).

Overwhelming Aura

- The vampyre can choose to overwhelm the aura of a victim and paralyze them into inaction. The vampyre must be in direct contact with the victim.
- Roll JDG SC (Target 15). Costs (-3) Soul Pool.
- Paralysis lasts for one minute (Success +1 to +5), ten minutes (Success +6 to +15), or one hour (Success +16 or more).

Feed from the Crowd

- When surrounded by a crowd with high emotions, the vampyre can feed indirectly.
- Roll JDG SC (Target 10). Costs (-1) Soul Pool.
- Vampyre draws (1) Soul Pool per minute from the crowd. This energy can be used to heal the life pool (per Vampyre Healing), but not the Soul Pool.

Create Thrall

- Can create permanent thrall who is their follower/slave. A thrall is created from a victim who is currently under the Emotion Control effect from the vampyre.
- Roll JDG SC (Target 20). Costs (-5) Soul Pool.
- If the attempt succeeds, the victim makes a JDG OC save, versus the original Thrall roll. If the victim fails, they become a permanent thrall of the undead vampyre.

The undead vampire also gains the following bonuses:

Vampyre Healing

- When the character feeds, they make a JDG healing roll, and it applies to **both** Life Pool and Soul Pool.
- To heal Life Pool: the character gains (+5) to the RESULTS of the healing roll per Soul Pool drained.
- To heal Soul Pool: the character gains (+10) to the RESULTS of the healing roll per Soul Pool drained.
- *For instance, if the character consumed three Soul Pool directly from a victim to feed, they would make a JDG-based healing roll, and apply the results to both the Life Pool and Soul Pool, with the following modifiers: (+15) to Life Pool and (+30) to Soul Pool.*

Beautiful Beast

- The character gains a (+30) permanent modifier to **Influence: Deception**. *NOTE: if the character is moving from Living to Undead vampyre, the character only gains (+10) to Influence: Deception.*

Naturally Skilled (does not apply to the character going from Living to Undead vampyre)

- Character gains (+20) permanent modifier to **Influence: Negotiation** and **(Survival) Stealth: Crowds**.
- Character gains (+40) permanent modifier to **(Esoteric) Mythological: Vamps**.

Infect Victim

- The bite of an undead vampyre can infect other humans.
- If an undead vampyre directly feeds from a victim, the victim has a low chance of becoming a new vampire. The victim makes an LCK SC (Target 5). If the victim fails, they become an immature vampyre.
- If an undead vampyre *chooses* to infect one of their victims, they must roll a JDG SC (Target 20). Costs (-5) Soul Pool. If successful, the victim makes an LCK SC (Target 20) to avoid infection.

Vitality in Death

- (+30) Life Pool [only gain (+10) Life Pool if moving from Living to Undead vampyre]
- (+60) Soul Pool [only gain (+20) Soul Pool if moving from Living to Undead vampyre]

The undead vampyre also gains the following weaknesses:

Soulfrenzy

- If an undead vampyre takes any Life Pool damage, they must make a JDG SC (Target 20) to avoid entering soulfrenzy.
- If they fail the roll, they will immediately attack anyone around them to feed, starting with wounded beings. The soulfrenzy vampire must make another JDG SC (Target 25) to avoid attacking friends, allies, and team members.

Photosensitivity

- The character takes (-30) Life Pool damage *per round* when exposed to direct sunlight or strong UV light.
- The character takes (-10) Life Pool damage *per round* when exposed to any sunlight or UV rays.

Silver

- Vampyres react negatively to silver, as it is considered a "pure" metal.
- Direct silver contact on the body will negate the Regeneration Talent.
- Silver weapons add 3(+10) total damage to any attack on the vampyre.

Wood

- Wood that is lodged in the heart will negate the Regeneration Talent.
- Wood that is lodged through the heart and into the earth will cause complete paralysis to the vampyre, and negate the Regeneration Talent.

Unaware while feeding

- When an undead vampyre feeds, they become completely unaware of their surroundings.

Faith Symbols

- If the wearer has sincere faith in a faith symbol, that faith symbol will repel or injure a vampyre.
- Vampyre receives a (-30) conditional modifier to approach or attack a faith symbol bearer.
- Vampyre is burned when touched by an active faith symbol and takes (-30) Life Pool damage from each contact.
- *Examples include: A cross for a Christian, a star of David for an orthodox Jew, a pentacle for a Wiccan, or even a compass for a Mason.*

THERIANTHROPE

Therianthropes are human shapeshifters with a hybrid virus that has ties to the same nightmare realm as the vamps, *Coşmar*. Playable therianthropes are restricted to land-based mammals (otters are ok, dolphins and whales are not). Therianthropes are divided into Predators and Prey animals, and further divided into Large and Small. As a therianthrope, figure out your character's beast (predator or prey, and large or small), and then the age stage. Start with the Age Stages below.

Therianthropes are forced to transform when exposed to the light of the full moon. For the one night per month when the moon is 100% full, every therianthrope is going to feel the almost-irresistible impulse to let their beast free. Any exposure to the light of a full moon will trigger the change. This means staying inside (no windows) or deep underground will mean Beast doesn't appear.

Younger therianthropes will feel the impulse on the nights surrounding the true full moon, and they will be forced to change on those nights as well. Older therianthropes can eventually control their impulses to only change on full moon days.

If a therianthrope stays away from the light of the full moon, the impulses get stronger and stronger. Each night after they refuse to change under the moonlight, they run the risk of changing spontaneously. If they are exposed to any moonlight after the full moon, they will usually change and let their beast run free. Some of the older therianthropes can resist the change for a while, but it always eventually becomes too much to resist.

When the full moon (or any moonlight) causes the therianthrope to change into their animal, the therianthrope cannot change back into a human until the dawn of the next morning.

Complete transformation into or out of their animal takes thirty seconds (fifteen rounds), and is painful for the 'thrope during the transformation. Partial transformation in either direction takes from ten to twenty seconds (five to ten rounds) and is extremely painful for the therianthrope.

For the therianthrope character, start with the age stage, and then choose the type of therianthrope.

Gruff is super chill, and always has munchies in his room. — G'Snoort

After they are infected, therianthropes only live for about twenty years. During that time, they go through five different age stages, ignoring any human age stages they pass through at the same time.

Immature Therianthrope

The immature therianthrope stage lasts until their first transformation at the next full moon. Until then the virus has not fully transformed the human, and the connection to *Coșmar* is not stable. It is during this time that the new 'thrope is struggling with their new beast. They also have a slim chance that they can be cured before the curse is permanent.

To cure an immature therianthrope, the link to the nightmare realm must be broken by killing the therianthrope sire/dam and then killing the virus, before the new therianthrope transforms for the first time. To kill the virus (after killing the sire/dam), the therianthrope must be subjected to a Faith Ability designed to further sever the connection to that realm. If both killing the sire/dam and the Faith Ability is completed before the immature therianthrope transforms for the first time, the curse is broken, and the human retains no remnants of the therianthrope curse.

The immature therianthrope cannot pass on the therianthrope infection to others.

The immature therianthrope gains one Talent.

Regeneration
- If a therianthrope takes damage to their Life Pool, the 'thrope starts to immediately draw from their Soul Pool on a 1:2 basis to regenerate their Life Pool and heal the damage.
- The therianthrope gains (+1) Life Pool/round, with a corresponding (-2) Soul Pool/round drain.
- The Regeneration occurs until the damage is healed or until the therianthrope reaches (0) Soul Pool.
- The therianthrope can choose to turn off the Regeneration by making a JDG SC (Target 15).

The immature therianthrope gains the following weaknesses:

Cannot Control the Beast
- The immature therianthrope cannot control when they change, and the first full moon will engage their beast change, regardless of their actual exposure to moonlight. If they are exposed to moonlight on either of the two days before the full moon, they will change.
- The immature therianthrope has no control over their beast when they are changed.

Silver
- Therianthropes react negatively to silver, as it is considered a "pure" metal.
- Direct silver contact on the body will negate the Regeneration Talent.
- Silver weapons add (+10) total damage to any attack on the immature therianthrope.

Aconitum Allergy

- Wolfsbane is a natural poison but is enhanced against therianthropes.
- Direct aconitum, or wolfsbane, contact on the body will negate the Regeneration Talent.
- Wolfsbane causes (-20) Life Pool damage when it touches an immature therianthrope.
- Ingesting wolfsbane causes (-80) Life Pool damage. Must be counteracted with an antidote before therianthrope will heal.

High-Frequency Noises

- Very loud noises above the normal human threshold of hearing will cause **Extreme Distraction** for two rounds (see the *Hidden Worlds Refined Core*).

YEARLING THERIANTHROPE

After their first transformation, the first year of the therianthrope is one where they are getting used to the beast within. They have begun to understand their beast and their new life. As a yearling, their animal form is slightly larger or slightly smaller than the natural size of their animal.

The full moon nights are considered the day before, the day of, and the day after the full moon. Each night's moon will cause transformation if exposed to the light.

The yearling therianthrope gains three Talents.

Regeneration

- If a therianthrope takes damage to their Life Pool, the 'thrope starts to immediately draw from their Soul Pool on a 1:1 basis to regenerate their Life Pool and heal the damage.
- The therianthrope gains (+1) Life Pool/round, with a corresponding (-1) Soul Pool/round drain.
- The Regeneration occurs until the damage is healed or until the therianthrope reaches (0) Soul Pool.
- The therianthrope can choose to turn off the Regeneration by making a JDG SC (Target 15).

Transformation

- The yearling therianthrope can change to their animal form at will.
- Changing back into human requires a JDG SC (Target 30). Costs (-3) Soul Pool. Cannot change back when transformed due to the full moon.

Control the Beast

- Roll JDG SC (Target 25).
- If successful, the yearling can control how their beast acts, except during the nights of the full moon.
- To control the beast during the nights of the full moon, roll a JDG SC (Target 35).

The yearling therianthrope gains the following bonuses:

- (+40) permanent modifier to **(Esoteric) Mythological: Therianthropes**
- (+20) Life Pool
- (+10) Soul Pool

Infect Victim

- The bite or scratch of a yearling therianthrope can infect other humans.
- If a yearling therianthrope directly bites or scratches a victim, the victim has a low chance of becoming a new therianthrope of the same type. The victim makes an LCK SC (Target 1). If the victim fails, they become an immature therianthrope.

The yearling therianthrope gains the following weakness:

Silver

- Therianthropes react negatively to silver, as it is considered a "pure" metal.
- Direct silver contact on the body will negate the Regeneration Talent.
- Silver weapons add +25 total damage to any attack on the yearling therianthrope.

Aconitum Allergy

- Wolfsbane is a natural poison but is enhanced against therianthropes.
- Direct aconitum contact on the body will negate the Regeneration Talent.
- Wolfsbane causes (-30) Life Pool damage when it touches a yearling therianthrope.
- Ingesting wolfsbane causes (-100) Life Pool damage. Must be counteracted with an antidote before therianthrope will heal.

High-Frequency Noises

- Very loud noises above the normal human threshold of hearing will cause **Extreme Distraction** for two rounds (see the *Hidden Worlds Refined Core*).

Mature Therianthrope

Mature therianthropes have lived with their beast for at least a year, up to around thirteen years as a 'thrope. The mature therianthrope is only subject to the full moon's power on the true full moon night. The mature therianthrope can change their beast's size up to, or down to, the size of the human side of the therianthrope.

The mature therianthrope gains four Talents:

Regeneration

- If a therianthrope takes damage to their Life Pool, the 'thrope starts to immediately draw from their Soul Pool on a 3:1 basis to regenerate their Life Pool and heal the damage.
- The therianthrope gains (+3) Life Pool/round, with a corresponding (-1) Soul Pool/round drain.
- The Regeneration occurs until the damage is healed or until the therianthrope reaches (0) Soul Pool.
- The therianthrope can choose to turn off the Regeneration by making a JDG SC (Target 15).

Transformation

- The mature therianthrope can change to their animal form at will.
- Changing back into human requires a JDG SC (Target 25). Costs (-1) Soul Pool. Cannot change back when transformed due to the full moon.

Control the Beast

- Roll JDG SC (Target 20).
- If successful, the mature therianthrope can control how their beast acts, except during the nights of the full moon.
- To control the beast during the nights of the full moon, roll a JDG SC (Target 25).

Partial Transformation

- Roll JDG SC (Target 20). Costs (-5) Soul Pool.
- The mature therianthrope can partially transform their body. They can change a whole limb, their upper torso, their lower torso, or their head. Each new set requires a roll.
- Roll JDG SC (Target 15) to change back. Costs (-1) Soul pool.

The mature therianthrope gains the following bonuses:

- (+60) permanent modifier to **(Esoteric) Mythological: Therianthropes** [Only (+20) if moving from Yearling to Mature]
- (+30) Life Pool [only gain (+10) Life Pool if moving from Yearling to Mature]
- (+20) Soul Pool [only gain (+10) Soul Pool if moving from Yearling to Mature]

Infect Victim

- The bite, scratch or blood of a mature therianthrope can infect other humans.
- If a mature therianthrope directly bites or scratches a victim or gets blood in an open wound of a victim, the victim has a low chance of becoming a new therianthrope of the same type. The victim makes an LCK SC (Target 5). If the victim fails, they become an immature therianthrope.

The mature therianthrope gains the following weakness:

Silver

- Therianthropes react negatively to silver, as it is considered a "pure" metal.
- Direct silver contact on the body will negate the Regeneration Talent.
- Silver weapons add 2(+10) total damage to any attack on the mature therianthrope.

Aconitum Allergy

- Wolfsbane is a natural poison but is enhanced against therianthropes.
- Direct aconitum contact on the body will negate the Regeneration Talent.
- Wolfsbane causes (-50) Life Pool damage when it touches a mature therianthrope.
- Ingesting wolfsbane causes (-125) Life Pool damage. Must be counteracted with an antidote before therianthrope will heal.

High-Frequency Noises

- Very loud noises above the normal human threshold of hearing will cause **Extreme Distraction** for two rounds (see the *Hidden Worlds Refined Core*).

Elder Therianthrope

Elder therianthropes have been dealing with their animal for over thirteen years. They are adept at controlling their beast, and are at their peak, only subject to the call of the full moon on the one night a month. The elder therianthrope can change their beast up to, or down to, the size of their human form.

The elder therianthrope gains four Talents:

Regeneration

- If a therianthrope takes damage to their Life Pool, the 'thrope starts to immediately draw from their Soul Pool on a 5:1 basis to regenerate their Life Pool and heal the damage.
- The therianthrope gains (+5) Life Pool/round, with a corresponding (-1) Soul Pool/round drain.
- The Regeneration occurs until the damage is healed or until the therianthrope reaches (0) Soul Pool.
- The therianthrope can choose to turn off the Regeneration by making a JDG SC (Target 15).

Transformation

- The elder therianthrope can change to their animal form at will.
- Changing back into human requires a JDG SC (Target 20). Costs (-1) Soul Pool. Cannot change back when transformed due to the full moon.

Control the Beast

- Roll JDG SC (Target 15).
- If successful, the elder therianthrope can control how their beast acts, except during the nights of the full moon.
- To control the beast during the nights of the full moon, roll a JDG SC (Target 20).

Partial Transformation

- Roll JDG SC (Target 15). Costs (-3) Soul Pool.
- The elder therianthrope can partially transform their body. They can change a whole limb, their upper torso, their lower torso, or their head. Each new set requires a roll.
- Roll JDG SC (Target 15) to change back. Costs (-1) Soul pool.

The elder therianthrope gains the following bonuses:

- (+60) permanent modifier to **(Esoteric) Mythological: Therianthropes** [Not applicable if moving from Mature to Elder]
- (+50) Life Pool [only gain (+20) Life Pool if moving from Mature to Elder]
- (+30) Soul Pool [only gain (+20) Soul Pool if moving from Mature to Elder]

Infect Victim

- The bite, scratch or blood of an elder therianthrope can infect other humans.
- If an elder therianthrope gets blood in an open wound of a victim, the victim has a low chance of becoming a new therianthrope of the same type. The victim makes an LCK SC (Target 10). If the victim fails, they become an immature therianthrope.
- If an elder therianthrope directly bites or scratches a victim, the victim has a chance to become infected as a therianthrope of the same type. The victim makes an LCK SC (Target 15). If the victim fails, they become an immature therianthrope.

The elder therianthrope gains the following weakness:

Silver
- Therianthropes react negatively to silver, as it is considered a "pure" metal.
- Direct silver contact on the body will negate the Regeneration Talent.
- Silver weapons add 3(+10) total damage to any attack on the elder therianthrope.

Aconitum Allergy
- Wolfsbane is a natural poison but is enhanced against therianthropes.
- Direct aconitum contact on the body will negate the Regeneration Talent.
- Wolfsbane causes (-50) Life Pool damage when it touches an elder therianthrope.
- Ingesting wolfsbane causes (-125) Life Pool damage. Must be counteracted with an antidote before therianthrope will heal.

High-Frequency Noises
- Very loud noises above the normal human threshold of hearing will cause **Extreme Distraction** for two rounds (see the *Hidden Worlds Refined Core*).

ANCIENT THERIANTHROPE

Ancient therianthropes are those who have lasted as a therianthrope for at least nineteen years. The average lifespan of a therianthrope is around twenty years, and the ancient therianthropes are close to their unnatural lifespans. The ancient therianthrope may live a few months or another year or two at the most. Ancient therianthropes can control the size of their beast up to, or down to, the size of their human form.

The ancient therianthrope gains four Talents:

Regeneration
- If a therianthrope takes damage to their Life Pool, the 'thrope starts to immediately draw from their Soul Pool on a 1:1 basis to regenerate their Life Pool and heal the damage.
- The therianthrope gains (+1) Life Pool/round, with a corresponding (-1) Soul Pool/round drain.
- The Regeneration occurs until the damage is healed or until the therianthrope reaches (0) Soul Pool.
- The therianthrope can choose to turn off the Regeneration by making a JDG SC (Target 15).

Transformation
- The ancient therianthrope can change to their animal form at will.
- Changing back into human requires a JDG SC (Target 10). Costs (-1) Soul Pool. Cannot change back when transformed due to the full moon.

Control the Beast
- Roll JDG SC (Target 10).
- If successful, the ancient therianthrope can control how their beast acts, except during the nights of the full moon.
- To control the beast during the nights of the full moon, roll a JDG SC (Target 15).

Partial Transformation

- Roll JDG SC (Target 10). Costs (-1) Soul Pool.
- The ancient therianthrope can partially transform their body. They can change a whole limb, their upper torso, their lower torso, or their head. Each new set requires a roll.
- Roll JDG SC (Target 10) to change back. Costs (-1) Soul pool.

The ancient therianthrope gains the following bonuses:

- (+60) permanent modifier to **(Esoteric) Mythological: Therianthropes** [Not applicable if moving from Elder to Ancient]
- (+50) Life Pool [do not gain any Life Pool if moving from Elder to Ancient]
- (+30) Soul Pool [do not gain any Soul Pool if moving from Elder to Ancient]

Infect Victim

- The bite, scratch or blood of an ancient therianthrope can infect other humans.
- If an ancient therianthrope gets blood in an open wound of a victim, the victim has a low chance of becoming a new therianthrope of the same type. The victim makes an LCK SC (Target 10). If the victim fails, they become an immature therianthrope.
- If an ancient therianthrope directly bites or scratches a victim, the victim has a chance to become infected as a therianthrope of the same type. The victim makes an LCK SC (Target 20). If the victim fails, they become an immature therianthrope.

The ancient therianthrope gains the following weakness:

Silver

- Therianthropes react negatively to silver, as it is considered a "pure" metal.
- Direct silver contact on the body will negate the Regeneration Talent.
- Silver weapons add 5(+10) total damage to any attack on the ancient therianthrope.

Aconitum Allergy

- Wolfsbane is a natural poison but is enhanced against therianthropes.
- Direct aconitum contact on the body will negate the Regeneration Talent.
- Wolfsbane causes (-50) Life Pool damage when it touches an elder therianthrope.
- Ingesting wolfsbane causes (-125) Life Pool damage. Must be counteracted with an antidote before therianthrope will heal.

High-Frequency Noises

- Very loud noises above the normal human threshold of hearing will cause **Extreme Distraction** for two rounds (see the *Hidden Worlds Refined Core*).

Ever heard of a dog whistle?
Yeah. It hurts the furry ones.
And some of us fae as well.
— G'Snoort

Therianthrope Type - Step 2

When choosing the therianthrope's beast, there are factors to consider. Will the therianthrope be large or small, and will they be changed by a predator or prey? While for the sake of play, the choice is limited to a land-based animal, there are useful characteristics as well as weaknesses to consider depending on the therianthrope. While predators are likely more perceived as fighters with claws and teeth, many prey have natural defenses with sheer size, antlers, hooves, or natural camouflage.

Choose the predator or prey below, including the specific animal.

LARGE PREDATOR

Some examples of large predators are: Wolves and large canines, lions and other large cats, bears, large boars, other pigs, and hippopotamus.

Use the following chart to change the character's attributes:

Current	New MIG	New HEA	New JDG	New ITL
1	8	5	1	1
2	8	5	1	1
3	8	5	2	1
4	9	6	2	2
5	9	6	3	2
6	10	7	3	3
7	11	8	4	3
8	12	9	4	3
9	13	10	5	4
10	15	12	5	4
11	16	13	6	4
12	17	14	6	4
13	18	15	7	5
14	19	16	7	5
15	20	17	8	5
16	20	17	9	6
17	21	18	10	6
18	22	19	11	7
19	23	20	12	7
20	25	22	13	8

Large predators also gain the following bonuses:

Teeth and Claws
- The predator's Base Strike damage from a bite attack is changed to 2(+10).
- The predator's Base Strike damage from their claw attacks is changed to 3(+15).

Predatory Skills

- (+10) permanent modifier to **Combat**
- (+30) permanent modifier to **(Combat) Melee: Claws**
- (+30) permanent modifier to **Survival: Track**

Heightened Senses (when transformed)

- Heightened Smell – (+15) conditional modifier to Survival: Awareness when using the sense of smell
- Low Light Vision – the predator can see in low-light conditions, but only in black and white, no colors if the area is dark enough.

Large predators also gain the following weaknesses:

Environmental Reticence

- The large predator has a problem with rapidly changing environments/settings.
- The predator receives a (-15) conditional modifier to all rolls when the environment changes too rapidly or drastically.

Ravenous Hunger

- The large predator must consume a larger than normal amount of food, especially after transforming. If not, they can start to be distracted by hunger. (See **Distracted** in the *Hidden Worlds Refined Core*).

SMALL PREDATOR

Some examples of small predators are: Hyenas and other mid-size dogs, small cats, ferrets, wolverines, badgers, mongoose, skunks, and raccoons.

Use the following chart to change the character's attributes:

Current	New HEC	New JDG	New MIG	New HEA
1	8	5	1	1
2	8	5	1	1
3	8	5	2	1
4	9	6	2	2
5	9	6	3	2
6	10	7	3	3
7	11	8	4	3
8	12	9	4	3
9	13	10	5	4
10	15	12	5	4
11	16	13	6	4
12	17	14	6	4
13	18	15	7	5
14	19	16	7	5
15	20	17	8	5
16	20	17	9	6
17	21	18	10	6
18	22	19	11	7
19	23	20	12	7
20	25	22	13	8

Small predators also gain the following bonuses:

Teeth and Claws
- The predator's Base Strike damage from a bite attack is changed to 2(+2).
- The predator's Base Strike damage from their claw attacks is changed to 2(+15).

Predatory Skills
- (+10) permanent modifier to **Athletics**
- (+30) permanent modifier to **(Combat) Melee: Claws**
- (+30) permanent modifier to **Survival: Stealth**

Heightened Senses (when transformed)
- Heightened Smell – (+15) conditional modifier to Survival: Awareness when using the sense of smell
- Low Light Vision – the predator can see in low-light conditions, but only in black and white, no colors if the area is dark enough.

Small predators also gain the following weaknesses:

Nocturnal Insomnia
- The small predator has a problem sleeping at night.
- Due to lack of sleep, the small predator can become irritable easily. They receive a (-5) permanent modifier to **Influence**.

Ravenous Hunger
- The small predator must consume a larger than normal amount of food, especially after transforming. If not, they can start to be distracted by hunger. (See **Distracted** in the *Hidden Worlds Refined Core*).

LARGE PREY

Large prey animal examples are: Elephants, cows and other bovine, moose, horses and other equine, rhinos, deer, and mountain and other goats.

Use the following chart to change the character's attributes:

Current	New MIG	New HEA	New JDG	New QCK
1	8	5	1	1
2	8	5	1	1
3	8	5	2	1
4	9	6	2	2
5	9	6	3	2
6	10	7	3	3
7	11	8	4	3
8	12	9	4	3
9	13	10	5	4
10	15	12	5	4
11	16	13	6	4
12	17	14	6	4
13	18	15	7	5
14	19	16	7	5
15	20	17	8	5
16	20	17	9	6
17	21	18	10	6
18	22	19	11	7
19	23	20	12	7
20	25	22	13	8

Large prey also gain the following bonuses:

Natural Attack
- The prey's Base Strike damage from their natural attack is changed to 3(+15).

Natural Skills

- (+10) permanent modifier to **Survival**
- (+20) permanent modifier to **(Combat) Melee: [Natural Attack]**
- (+40) permanent modifier to **Survival: Awareness**

Natural Armor (when transformed)

- Large prey gains natural armor when transformed: –/50/50

Large prey also gain the following weaknesses:

Panics Easily

- The large prey gets panicked too easily. When startled, roll JDG SC (Target 23).
- If they fail, the large prey receives the **Panicked** condition for 2 rounds.

Ravenous Hunger

- The large prey must consume a larger than normal amount of food, especially after transforming. If not, they can start to be distracted by hunger. (See **Distracted** in the *Hidden Worlds Refined Core*).

SMALL PREY

Examples of small prey are: Rabbits, gerbils and other rodents, chihuahua and other toy dogs, chinchillas, squirrels, otters, porcupines, and pika.

Use the following chart to change the character's attributes:

Current	New QCK	New HEC	New HEA	New MIG
1	8	5	1	1
2	8	5	1	1
3	8	5	2	1
4	9	6	2	2
5	9	6	3	2
6	10	7	3	3
7	11	8	4	3
8	12	9	4	3
9	13	10	5	4
10	15	12	5	4
11	16	13	6	4
12	17	14	6	4
13	18	15	7	5
14	19	16	7	5
15	20	17	8	5
16	20	17	9	6
17	21	18	10	6
18	22	19	11	7
19	23	20	12	7
20	25	22	13	8

Small prey also gain the following bonuses:

Natural Attack

- The prey's Base Strike damage from their natural attack is changed to 2(+15).

Natural Skills

- (+10) permanent modifier to **Athletics**
- (+20) permanent modifier to **(Combat) Melee: [Natural Attack]**
- (+40) permanent modifier to **Survival: Stealth**

Natural Camouflage (when transformed)

- Small prey gains natural camouflage when transformed: (+25) conditional modifier to Survival: Stealth

Small prey also gain the following weaknesses:

Panics Easily

- The small prey gets panicked too easily. When startled, roll JDG SC (Target 23).
- If they fail, the small prey receives the **Panicked** condition for 2 rounds.

Attention Deficit, Ooooh Shiny

- The small prey gains the trait **Attention Deficit, Ooooh Shiny (ADOS)**. (See **Attention Deficit, Ooooh Shiny** in the *Hidden Worlds Refined Core*).

CORRUPTED

The corrupted at one time served one of the elder gods from the horror-filled eldritch realm called *Rhy'ctharn*. What started as cult worship eventually became a journey to corruption. The human cult worshiper accepted the power and connection to their gods, absorbing the eldritch energy and letting it twist and corrupt them. They eventually found a way out of the cult, but their corruption still ties them to *Rhy'ctharn*.

Eldritch Power: The eldritch power of a redeemed corrupted is a double-edged blade. It gives them the power to fight against the cults and the corrupted who are pushing for the elder gods to return. It also has the potential to draw the attention and ire of the eldritch powers they no longer serve.

Eldritch Transmutation: The corrupted can use their eldritch connection to temporarily transmute their form into something dark and twisted. Some of the corrupted become horribly twisted beasts called Animus, while others become shadowy forms of darkness called Draeden. Both forms survive in darkness and are driven away by the light of the sun.

Every time a corrupted transforms into their corrupted state, they run the risk of becoming stuck in that state until the sun rises again.

- To transform to the corrupted state, roll a JDG SC (Target 10). Costs (-2) Soul Pool.

- To transmute back to human, the effort gets more difficult every time, resetting when the sun rises every morning. It costs (-1) Soul Pool each time they transmute back to human.

  - The first time each day the corrupted tries to transmute back to human, roll a JDG SC (Target 5).
  - Each additional transmutation back that day, add (+5) to the JDG target. *For instance, the second time, the character would roll a JDG SC (Target 10), the third time would be a (Target 15), the fourth a (Target 20), and so forth.*
  - If the corrupted fails a roll to transmute back to human, they are stuck in that form until the next sunrise.

Eldritch Banishment: The eldritch form can be banished back to *Rhy'ctharn* with the right faith ability, or by another corrupted. If banished, the eldritch form cannot be called by the human corrupted until the next sunset.

Eldritch Attention: If the corrupted fail to transmute out of their form before the next sunrise, they have the chance of drawing the attention of their eldritch gods. If the eldritch gods actually notice the errant corrupted, the horrors will send their cultist followers and other corrupted to bring the redeemed back into eldritch service.

The Final Chance: If a corrupted loses enough Soul Pool to drop to (-10) Soul Pool, the corrupted has a chance of becoming a puppet of the eldritch horrors.

- Roll JDG SC (Target 35) to avoid having their corrupted form taken over as a mindless minion of the eldritch gods. If they fail, they become overwhelmed by the eldritch enemy and become a mindless puppet of the eldritch horrors (the character is effectively a permanent NPC).

- If the corrupted is successful on the SC, the corrupted becomes catatonic until healed from (-10) Soul Pool.
- If the corrupted uses a destiny point to avoid the trigger/SC, the corrupted still becomes catatonic until healed from (-10) Soul Pool.

All corrupted gain the following weaknesses:

Change is Pain
- Transmutation to or from the eldritch form is painful for the corrupted.
- The transmutation takes two rounds (four seconds) to complete the transmutation.
- During that time, the corrupted gains the **Minor Distraction** condition.

Born of Night
- Any corrupted transmutation is immediately changed back into their human form when any part of their body/form is exposed to any daylight.

Null Faith
- Any transmuted corrupted that is hit with a null faith field or ability must roll a JDG SC (Target 30-50 – based on the strength of the field). If they fail the SC, they gain the **Medium Distraction** condition while in the field. If they fail by at least (-10), the character is immediately transmuted back to human and suffers **Major Distraction** for two rounds, then **Medium Distraction** while they remain in the field.

ANIMUS

The Animus is the physical manifestation of the corrupted. Each corrupted form is visually different, however, they all share some characteristics.

- The body form of the corrupted grows to human giant size.
- The skin thickens and roughens, looking like the mottled green skin of a cephalopod.
- The arms extend into longer tentacles with cephalopod-like suckers, and the fingers extend into individual smaller tentacles.
- The head becomes misshapen, matching the skin, and the eyes glow with a deep fluorescent green.

Use the following chart to change the character's attributes:

Current	New MIG	New QCK	New JDG	New LCK
1	8	5	1	1
2	8	5	1	1
3	8	5	2	1
4	9	6	2	2
5	9	6	3	2
6	10	7	3	3
7	11	8	4	3
8	12	9	4	3
9	13	10	5	4
10	15	12	5	4
11	16	13	6	4
12	17	14	6	4
13	18	15	7	5
14	19	16	7	5
15	20	17	8	5
16	20	17	9	6
17	21	18	10	6
18	22	19	11	7
19	23	20	12	7
20	25	22	13	8

The animus corrupted gains four Talents:

Eldritch Transmutation
- Roll a JDG SC (Target 10) to transmute form to Animus. Costs (-2) Soul Pool.
- Base Strike Damage changes to 3(+15).
- Animus form gains natural armor: –/100/100
- Fear Aura. Any non-friend/non-party within visual range (2) gains the **Scared** condition.
- To transmute back, roll a JDG SC (Target 5) the first time each day. Costs (-1) Soul Pool. Target number adds (+5) every additional time transmuting back. Resets at sunrise every day.

Corrupted Healing (When Transmuted)

- Roll a JDG SC (Target 20). Costs (-5) Soul Pool.
- Corrupted must be touching the target.
- Drain (-10) Soul Pool per round from the target, and gain (+5) Life Pool per round
- Talent stops when contact is broken

Eldritch Banishment (When Not Transmuted)

- Roll a JDG SC (Target 20). Costs (-5) Soul Pool.
- Requires physical contact with eldritch form.
- If Successful, the target makes JDG SC (Target 35) to remain in this realm.
- Corrupted eldritch forms are banished until the next sunset. Eldritch horrors direct from *Rhy'ctharn* are banished back to that realm and must be re-summoned to this realm.

Eldritch Sense

- Corrupted can sense when they are around other corrupted, or eldritch horrors, even when they are hiding their true form. GM Discretion applies.

The animus corrupted gains the following bonuses:

- (+20) permanent modifier to **Combat**
- (+30) permanent modifier to **Combat: Unarmed**
- (+40) permanent modifier to **(Esoteric) Cult: [Specific Cult/Horror]**

DRAEDEN

The Draeden is the metaphysical manifestation of the eldritch power coursing through their body. The draeden becomes a mere shadow of their human body. They become a shadow-like form and are unable to physically interact with the realm. This also means they cannot be attacked with normal weapons.

Use the following chart to change the character's attributes:

Current	New JDG	New QCK	New MIG	New LCK
1	8	5	1	1
2	8	5	1	1
3	8	5	2	1
4	9	6	2	2
5	9	6	3	2
6	10	7	3	3
7	11	8	4	3
8	12	9	4	3
9	13	10	5	4
10	15	12	5	4
11	16	13	6	4
12	17	14	6	4
13	18	15	7	5
14	19	16	7	5
15	20	17	8	5
16	20	17	9	6
17	21	18	10	6
18	22	19	11	7
19	23	20	12	7
20	25	22	13	8

The draeden corrupted gains four Talents:

Shadow Form
- Roll a JDG SC (Target 10). Costs (-2) Soul Pool
- Dresden is impervious to all non-faith-based damage as a being of shadow.
- Other than verbal communication, they cannot interact with the natural world outside without using a faith-based ability.
- While in Shadow Form, the draeden gains a (+20) conditional modifier to all Faith: Cast SCs.
- While in Shadow Form, all faith abilities cast have Drain/2 (round down, minimum 1).
- Fear Aura. Any non-friend/non-party within visual range (2) gains the **Scared** condition.
- To transmute back, roll a JDG SC (Target 5) the first time each day. Costs (-1) Soul Pool. Target number adds (+5) every additional time transmuting back. Resets at sunrise every day.

Soul Burn (When Transmuted)
- Roll a JDG SC (Target 30). Costs (-10) Soul Pool
- The draeden corrupted have the ability to directly attack the souls of their enemies.
- The draeden must be "touching" the target with their shadow form.
- When successful, the target must make a JDG OC (Target original roll) to avoid Soul Burn.
- If the target fails, the target takes (-30) Soul Pool damage.

Eldritch Banishment (When Not Transmuted)
- Roll a JDG SC (Target 20). Costs (-5) Soul Pool.
- Requires physical contact with eldritch form.
- If Successful, the target makes JDG SC (Target 35) to remain in this realm.
- Corrupted eldritch forms are banished until the next sunset. Eldritch horrors direct from *Rhy'ctharn* are banished back to that realm and must be re-summoned to this realm.

Eldritch Sense
- Corrupted can sense when they are around other corrupted, or eldritch horrors, even when they are hiding their true form. GM Discretion applies.

The draeden corrupted gains the following bonuses:

- (+20) permanent modifier to **Faith**
- (+15) permanent modifier to **Faith: Cast**
- (+15) permanent modifier to **Faith: Resist**
- (+40) permanent modifier to **(Esoteric) Cult: [Specific Cult/Horror]**

EXPERIMENTS

The experiments are those humans who have been fundamentally altered by chemical or genetic experimentation. Whether the result of an involuntary experiment, a voluntary opportunity, or an exploration of self-experimentation, the humans that are experimented on are irrevocably changed.

All experiments gain three Talents:

Push Beyond

- Activate at will - takes one combat action.
- Combine both Life Pool and Soul Pool into one temporary Combined Pool.
- Gain a (+25) conditional modifier to all physical-based skills.
- Roll a JDG SC (Target 25) to deactivate.
- When deactivated, split the remaining Combined Pool equally into the Life Pool and Soul Pool. Neither Pool can be refilled higher than the maximum pool.

Escape Artist

- Roll a JDG SC (Target 20). Costs (-5) Soul Pool.
- Escape any confining factor. This includes such factors as mind control, cages, rooms, restraints, etc.

Fearless

- Experiments have been exposed to the horrors of humanity, and they process fear differently than most, pushing through where others falter. They only have a maximum of **Scared** for Fear conditions.

GENE-SPLICED

The gene-spliced experiments have had their human DNA mixed with the DNA of another terrestrial creature. Gene-spliced humans are prevalent in science fiction, with such examples as the human fly and those creatures that Dr. Moreau experimented on. Gene-splicing is permanent.

The Creature: When a human gene sequence is spliced with a creature, they take on some of the characteristics of the creature. This includes both the strengths and weaknesses of the creature.

Physical Characteristics: A gene-spliced experiment is now spliced with another creature, gaining some of that creature's characteristics. This includes distinguishing physical characteristics that are very evident to observers.

Experiments change their attributes based on their transformations. Choose which two attributes are the strengths of the character, based on their heritage, and which three attributes are their lowest, again based on their experiment.

- Pick an attribute to be your character's best attribute based on their experiment then compare the roll of the d20 to the HIGH 1 column
- Pick a second to be your character's next best, again based on their experiment then compare the roll of the d20 to the HIGH 2 column
- Pick an attribute to be your character's weakest, then compare the roll of the d20 to the Low 1 column
- Pick an attribute to be your character's next weakest, then compare the roll of the d20 to the Low 2 column

- Pick an attribute to be your character's least weakest, then compare the roll of the d20 to the Low 3 column

Gene-spliced experiments gain one additional talent:

ROLL	High (1)	High (2)	Normal	Normal	Normal	Low (3)	Low (2)	Low (1)
1	8	5	1	1	1	1	1	1
2	8	5	2	2	2	1	1	1
3	8	5	3	3	3	2	2	1
4	9	6	4	4	4	2	2	2
5	9	6	5	5	5	3	3	2
6	10	7	6	6	6	3	3	3
7	11	8	7	7	7	4	4	3
8	12	9	8	8	8	5	4	3
9	13	10	9	9	9	6	5	4
10	15	12	10	10	10	7	5	4
11	16	13	11	11	11	8	6	4
12	17	14	12	12	12	9	6	4
13	18	15	13	13	13	10	7	5
14	19	16	14	14	14	11	7	5
15	20	17	15	15	15	12	8	5
16	20	17	16	16	16	13	9	6
17	21	18	17	17	17	14	10	6
18	22	19	18	18	18	15	11	7
19	23	20	19	19	19	16	12	7
20	25	22	20	20	20	17	13	8

Creature Comforts

- Pick an important trait of whatever creature has been spliced with the character. The character gains the associated advantages and disadvantages of the trait. If there are damage figures or other mechanical limitations,
- *For example: Gills from a shark would allow the character to breathe underwater, but they can only breathe underwater and require a rebreather for out-of-water living. The hairs on the hands/arms and feet/legs would give a character the spider's ability to walk on walls, but the character's arms and legs would be all covered in spines. The character might want the powerful claws of a tiger, but they would also have massive permanent murder mittens.*

Gene-spliced experiments gain the following bonuses:

- (+10) permanent modifier to **Survival**
- (+20) permanent modifier to **Survival: Awareness**
- (+20) permanent modifier to **Survival: Forage**
- (+30) permanent modifier to **(Athletics) Movement: [Specific Creature Movement]**
- (+25) Soul Pool

NOTE: Characters changed during gameplay, after character creation, do not get the skill-based bonuses.

CHEMICAL

Chemical experiments are those humans who have ingested an addictive and dangerous combination of custom chemicals to change their physical and metaphysical realities. Chemical experiments are often found in science fiction and include such characters as Dr. Jekyll/Mr. Hyde, Bane, and the Invisible Man. Chemical experimentation is irrevocable.

The Chemical: Chemical experiments are highly addicted to their chemical compounds. The chemical compounds also change their physiology and metaphysical reality permanently enough that their body requires a constant infusion of the chemical to maintain. The effects of the chemicals are only temporary, and the experiment's body requires them to survive.

If the character goes without their required daily dose of the chemical, they receive a (-30) conditional modifier to all SC and OC attempts until they get their daily dose.

The Supply: Finding and creating stockpiles of their custom compounds can be a problem for the experiment. While the benefits are great, the trouble of keeping supplies handy can be very troublesome for the chemically dependent experiment.

Experiments change their attributes based on their transformations. Choose which two attributes are the strengths of the character, based on their heritage, and which three attributes are their lowest, again based on their experiment.

- Pick an attribute to be your character's best attribute based on their experiment then compare the roll of the d20 to the HIGH 1 column
- Pick a second to be your character's next best, again based on their experiment then compare the roll of the d20 to the HIGH 2 column
- Pick an attribute to be your character's weakest, then compare the roll of the d20 to the Low 1 column
- Pick an attribute to be your character's next weakest, then compare the roll of the d20 to the Low 2 column
- Pick an attribute to be your character's least weak, then compare the roll of the d20 to the Low 3 column

ROLL	High (1)	High (2)	Normal	Normal	Normal	Low (3)	Low (2)	Low (1)
1	8	5	1	1	1	1	1	1
2	8	5	2	2	2	1	1	1
3	8	5	3	3	3	2	2	1
4	9	6	4	4	4	2	2	2
5	9	6	5	5	5	3	3	2
6	10	7	6	6	6	3	3	3
7	11	8	7	7	7	4	4	3
8	12	9	8	8	8	5	4	3
9	13	10	9	9	9	6	5	4
10	15	12	10	10	10	7	5	4
11	16	13	11	11	11	8	6	4
12	17	14	12	12	12	9	6	4
13	18	15	13	13	13	10	7	5
14	19	16	14	14	14	11	7	5
15	20	17	15	15	15	12	8	5
16	20	17	16	16	16	13	9	6
17	21	18	17	17	17	14	10	6
18	22	19	18	18	18	15	11	7
19	23	20	19	19	19	16	12	7
20	25	22	20	20	20	17	13	8

Chemical experiments gain one additional Talent:

Chemical Enhancement

- Choose the major effect that is caused by your chemical formula.
- The chemical compound can be ingested as a liquid, solid, or gas.
- This trick also has a massive downside.
- *For Example: If the formula turns the character invisible, it does not make their clothes invisible. If the formula makes their skin as hard as rock, they also weigh as much as that much rock. If they can turn to smoke, a strong wind could blow them around.*
- Recommend not picking things like super strength, super speed, super intelligence, etc as these are better represented by having high attributes in those areas.

Chemical experiments gain the following bonuses:

- (+10) permanent modifier to **Survival**
- (+20) permanent modifier to **Medical: First Aid**
- (+50) permanent modifier to **(Survival) Forage: (Addictive Chemical)**
- (+25) Soul Pool

NOTE: Characters changed during gameplay, after character creation, do not get the skill-based bonuses.

GAMEMASTER
CHAPTER FOUR

As a GameMaster, the Other Handbook can be both a boon and a burden. As a boon, the Other Handbook provides the rules for your players to create amazing Other-based characters. On the other hand, those amazing Other-based characters can wreak havoc on your carefully crafted campaign unless you plan for the chaos that Others bring to the table.

TIPS FOR CREATING OTHERS

As a GM, it is up to you to help your players choose and create their Other characters. As always, start with that Session 0, which allows you to set the standards for the campaign. When a player wants to create an Other character, there are several points that can help them, and you, figure out where they want to go with their character.

- Created or Changed?

    - What Playable Other are they going to build?
    - If they are a Changed Other, how old were they when they were changed?
    - How long have they been an Other?

- What have they been doing?

    - Do they hold a position in society?
    - Are they in hiding?

- Is there something in their background that could be problematic? Powerful enemies? No experience in the world? Wanted by the OTA for Sanction?

- Is this player's Other character the only one in the group? Is there a mix? Are they all Others?

Once you work through those questions, you can move forward based on the entire group makeup. Below, we cover the following topics: Balancing Others and Humans and Running an Others-only Game.

BALANCING OTHERS AND HUMANS

One of the most difficult parts of having Others in your game is balancing the game to encompass the differences between the Others and standard humans. The temptation might be to either gimp the Others or to boost the humans to keep up, but neither of those options serves the game balance well.

There are some very large factors necessary to balance a game with humans and Others:

- Skill Balance
- Power (Attribute) Creep
- Talents and Bonuses
- External Forces

Skill Balance can be a major problem, especially if your player is building a vampire or long-lived cryptid or construct. When a vampire or cryptid has been around for over a hundred years, the skillset will normally be an order of magnitude higher than a character who has only been around for ten years or less in their career.

I recommend working with the Other player and limiting their time in their career with some of the following factors.

- **Career in Hiding:** Point out to the player that it is usually pretty hard for an Other to openly live and work in a society when they have to hide their nature.

  - Is the character a vampire? When they have to avoid daylight, it is awfully difficult to maintain a solid career. Especially if they have had to move often to avoid being hunted. Maybe suggest that they only count the years as half or one-third of the time that would normally count in their career.
  - Is the character a cryptid? Where have they been working so that they can stay in hiding while gaining career experience? I would recommend counting their time in their career as about one-third or one-fourth of the normal time in career.

- **Career Variety:** Recommend the character has bounced around to a lot of different careers, which offer different skill sets.

- **Expertise is Your Friend:** As the character gains bunches of points, make sure they are spending some of them on what would normally be considered "Obsolete Skills" - skills that they would have learned during a time when technology has changed vastly.

  - If they have been a mechanic in transportation for a long time, a large amount of their expertise should be in classic/older cars or even horse-drawn carriages.

Power (Attribute) Creep can be another one of those balance breakers. The Playable Others are the only PCs in the game that can have Attributes max out above (20). While this may seem to be something that might break the balance of the party, there are two key principles to keep in mind.

First, those same characters that may have two or three Attributes above (20), also are limited by at least one, two, or three Attributes that are limited far below (20). At least one of those attributes is limited to no more than (8). This has been shown in testing to do a good job of balancing the attributes with normal humans.

The other method of making sure there is no power creep in the group is to make sure the normal humans in the group have different attributes that are higher than the Others. This is part of balancing the party and is why a Session 0 is so important. That session is where you can help make sure that everyone will get a chance to shine in the spotlight.

Talents and Bonuses are the final large factors that often cause concern when balancing Others and humans in a group. This should not be as much of a factor during gameplay, as each Other has large weaknesses as well. So how do I balance them?

If a character seems to be hogging the spotlight because of their utility, it is within your purview as the GM to tip the scales a bit by playing up to the character's weaknesses. Is the corrupted draeden rolling through all the bad guys too easily? Put a Null Faith field in their way. Is the vampire rolling through combat too easily? Add a puzzle to let the other PCs get a chance.

NOTE: This is the same advice for handling any overpowered character. The key is to have your adventures challenge all the PCs, not just the one.

External Forces can also become a limiting factor on the PCs. If the character is a vampire or dhampir, do they have obligations to a coven? If the character is a faeling, what does their Court think about what they are doing? If the PCs are part of an organization like the OTA, are there rules and laws that they have to follow? All of these external forces can have a major factor in helping to limit and balance the Others in a mixed group.

Other Negative Factors can also apply to balance the power of the Others. Some of those include:

- Lifespan changes cause major disruptions
- Loss of previous occupation and contacts
- Threat of losing humanity

Neuro's ok, and his wife makes awesome cookies!
— G'snoort

RUNNING AN OTHERS-ONLY GAME

If you are running a group with Others only, you will need to keep a couple of different factors in your mind as your group works through Session 0. First, understand that a group of Others-only is generally going to be a more powerful group than a similar group of humans-only. If you want to slow down or minimize some of the power creep issues listed above, you will want to be careful in crafting your campaign. Either the BBEGs get bigger and badder, or your players intentionally nerf their characters while building them.

 Another big factor to figure out during Session 0 is determining how all these disparate Others came together in a group. How would you put a sasquatch, a weregoat, and a vampire on the same team? This is where you, as the GM, have to get creative. An easy answer is for them to work for the Office of Transhuman Affairs or some other organization.

But what about having them be hired to solve a mystery plaguing one of the fae courts? This is where your Session 0 can really shine and set you up for a fun campaign.

> *Game story: When we first started talking about running the Mis-Adventures of the Restore Corps on my channel (https://www.youtube.com/one-leggedgm), we knew that we would be playing mostly with Others (testing out this very book). Instead of running a power game, I wanted to run a very different kind of Other game. We decided to run a more procedural/investigative campaign than a combat campaign. This meant we had to come up with a reason to put these characters on a lower team, and not a front-line combat team. We did this by really making them quirky and less powerful.*
>
> *A vampire that is allergic to blood? A computer tech sasquatch? A stoner weregoat? A seventeen-year-old half-dryad? Those were the characters that showcased the system, without simply power gaming through the campaign.*

WHAT ABOUT NATE?

Your Nate is going to ask why they cannot combine playable others into new, and terribly OP, variants (Bad Nate! No taco for you!). Here are some of the *in-game/story* reasons for this ban on variants.

Except for humans, who are really not tied to any realm, the various Others almost all come from different realms, and the realms generally do not mix. With humans being that exception, they are the only ones who can potentially be the host for another realm's energy. Fortunately, once a human becomes a host of another realm's connection, they cannot connect with a different realm.

When one of the demihumans is born, their hybrid connection to the Other realms prevents them from spreading their connection, and it also prevents them from procreating and having offspring. Because this realm connection is on the DNA level, hybrid humans are naturally sterile.

Cryptids maintain a strong connection to the Natural Earth Realm, which protects them from being connected to either of the darker realms. And humans and cryptids are not genetically compatible in any way, and therefore cannot breed together. In the vast majority of cases, cryptids and humans are completely incompatible.

The Fae are from *Álfheimer*, and the realm's energy keeps them protected from being overwhelmed by the Nightmare and Eldritch realms, although creatures from the Nightmare Realm can feed off the fae. Even within their own realm, most fae cannot cross breed, and it is only the realm-less nature of the humans that allows some fae to breed with humans. As mentioned before, the resulting progeny are sterile and remain immune from the corruption of the Nightmare and Eldritch Realms.

The gods from the various pantheon realms are much the same as the fae. Their own realms keep them protected from the corruption of the Nightmare and Eldritch realms, although they can become food for the denizens of the Nightmare realm. When a god connects with a human to breed a demigod, the resulting progeny are completely sterile and remain immune from the corruption of the Nightmare and Eldritch Realms.

The denizens of *Coşmar*, the Nightmare Realm, are twisted by that realm's dark energy and are immune to corruption from the Eldritch Realm. Vamps and Therianthropes are naturally sterile, as the dark energy has completely changed their DNA. The only way they can pass on the virus and create progeny is through the bites and scratches that act as natural transmission vectors.

The twisted horrors of *Rhy'ctharn*, the Eldritch Realm, are so corrupted that they are protected from any other realm's additional corruption. The corrupted creatures that use the dark energy are naturally sterile after the corruption, and can only assist others with connection to the eldritch realm through worship and sacrifice.

You will notice that I specifically did not mention the Experiments. While the experiments themselves are sterile due to their terrible circumstances, they are not protected from the other realm energies. This is the one point where I will break from the story reasoning and say that the experiments are specifically balanced for a human base character. The reason they cannot be combined with any of the other Others is that we said so. Do with that what you will.

> NOTE: No, Nate, I'm not changing my mind. You cannot have a chemical experiment-vampire.

STORY HOOKS

A few example story hooks are listed below so that you can use to build an encounter or even campaign around. Each one will easily involve Playable Others groups, either blended or Others-only.

MAD SCIENTIST

Demigods and faelings are disappearing all over the area. The Gray Court has approached the group to determine: Why are they disappearing? Who is behind it? Should they be concerned? The PCs quickly discover rumors that a science lab is behind the kidnappings, and they are experimenting on the missing demihumans.

- Science lab is corporate-funded under a variety of holding companies.
- The anti-Other corporation behind the science lab is working toward a new virus to wipe out fae and demigods.

FAMILY REQUEST

One of the party's family has a request. They would like an escort for a fragile family member to another family home/location. The fragile family member has control of a vast treasure appropriate to the Other, and a rival family member will stop at nothing to gain access to that treasure/knowledge. The PCs must get this fragile family member to their destination safely, and will face stiff opposition.

- Best with a Fae family connected to one of the Courts.
- The rival family has to not be identified to avoid repercussions with the Court.

THE HUNT

A powerful sasquatch clan has several members who go missing. One of the bodies shows up and shows evidence of being hunted. The PCs are asked to figure out what is happening.

- The PCs figure out a wealthy group of hunters has started hunting the sasquatch for sport.
- The hunters kidnap the squatch and take them to a remote island where they are hunted.
- Either the PCs will help the sasquatch clan track these hunters down and get revenge, or they will be hired to do so, to keep the clan out of the revenge business.

COMING APOCALYPSE

The PCs are investigating a cult for illegal activity. The cult turns out to be one small part of a conspiracy that reaches the upper echelons of society who are trying to summon an elder god to earth. The PCs can react in several ways, based on their resources and authority.

- The PCs can investigate further, slowly moving up the chain of cultists and cult leaders until they find the upper echelon.
- The PCs can work to stop the original cult, and work on the investigation laterally - playing whack-a-cult as they pop up, or they can work to shut down the connection to the Eldritch Realm wherever the connection is found.

WORLD OF THE OTHER
CHAPTER FIVE

Welcome to this briefing. I was asked by Director Kalafut to chat with you. Her department is responsible for intelligence and planning for missions, as well as determining Sanction Status for EIS agents. My name is Gigglesnoort, and while I'm normally assigned to help with the War Wagon in the motor pool, I was asked to brief you today. If you are one of the direct-action agents for the Office of Transhuman Affairs, Director Kalafut's teams will be developing the intel and parameters for your missions. If you are an Esoteric Interdiction Specialist, her teams determine the sanctions on human or esoteric threats.

In this briefing, we will cover an overview of the world of the Others. From vampires to fae, and pantheons to cryptids, this training may be what helps you survive as an agent for the Office of Transhuman Affairs or as an Esoteric Interdiction Specialist for a private firm.

SOCIETY OF THE FANG

Forget almost everything you know about vampires. Legends and popular media have described vampires, their powers, and their weaknesses. And most of it is wrong. While some of the misinformation is simply a misunderstanding, a lot of it is disinformation or propaganda disseminated by vampires and their minions.

ORIGINS OF VAMPS

While stories of demons and creatures drinking blood stretch back through the millennia, the scourge of modern vampires was unleashed on the world in the 1600s by the Unseelie Court. Wishing to curb the spread of humans from parts of Southeastern Europe, a group of dark fae captured a small group of human peasants and used ritual magic to open a gateway to another realm, inviting the dark energies to meld with the humans, turning them into monstrous weapons.

The energies from the nightmare realm called *Coșmar*, twisted the humans, making them violent monsters that fed in the night. As the new monsters began to infect more people, the infection from the nightmare realm evolved. Eventually, the soul-feeding vampyre evolved from their vampire cousins, and both the vampires and vampyres gained the ability to tolerate the sunlight somewhat, at least while they lived.

It was in the late 1600s that vampires and vampyres broke their connection to the Unseelie, and became the monsters they were destined to become.

"

VAMPS THROUGH THE AGES

From the 1400s through the present day, vampires and vampyres have lived in the darkness. While most vamps were monsters that were tracked down and killed by church-trained hunters, some "lived" long enough to become master vamps, gaining power and followers. These master vamps used their long lives to build the resources and followers to survive and thrive, becoming puppet masters behind the scenes and controlling their empires.

As technology and communications blossomed, vamps learned to embrace technology, using it to accomplish their plans and spread disinformation about the threat that vamps actually pose to humanity. As the vamps built their empires, they shunned any of the other so-called monsters, the Others. Vamp society tends to stand alone, not letting outsiders interfere with their society built on strength and power. Whether the strength is physical or political, the vamps who run their vamp society are ruthless dictators who keep a spiked gauntlet on the neck of their society.

THE MODERN VAMP

The modern vamp is a study of contrasts: Monsters of the night and pillars in the community. While the vast majority of vamps are the monsters of folklore, there is a core community of "civilized" vamps that form an entire society that operates in the shadows of the modern world. This society is engaged in a long-running war with humans and their mortal enemies, therianthropes.

THE CONCLAVE

Ancient Masters are those who have survived through the years, gaining power and followers. Found all over the civilized world, ancient master vamps use their political and economic power to wage a subtle war against humanity and therianthropes. As they wield their political and economic power over humans, they use their physical and metaphysical power to control the vamp societies they are protecting.

A small group of the most powerful ancient master vamps exercises this control through a secret council of ancients called the Conclave. This secret council contains both vampire and vampyre ancient masters and works to maintain order and control over the cities and covens throughout society. This hierarchy is what keeps some semblance of control in vamp society.

The Conclave communicates their directives to master and ancient master vamps who control the covens and city-states. When a local coven or group of vampires begins to cause enough trouble to draw the attention of the human authorities, the Conclave often sends their own enforcers to correct the situation, usually with lethal violence.

If a Conclave Master is destroyed, the rest of the Conclave proposes Enclave Master candidates based on power, and the top candidates are subjected to trials to determine if they are worthy of being elevated to Conclave Master. If an Enclave Master is not elevated after the trials, they are almost always ritually sacrificed, leaving a space in the hierarchy at the top of the Enclave to be filled.

ENCLAVES

Regional territories of vampires and vampyres are called Enclaves. Each Enclave is based around a major population center and is led by an ancient master vampire and an ancient master vampyre. Each Enclave Master is the direct conduit of the Conclave directions to their particular species, with the two supporting each other in their operations.

Enclave territory does not necessarily follow the lines of the maps, and the status of the Enclave is directly related to its importance in both vamp and human political influence. When an Enclave Master is destroyed, the Conclave will place a new Enclave Master directly in the leadership line.

Some of the largest Enclaves are found in:

- Greater Washington DC
- Greater New York City/Newark
- Miami
- Las Vegas
- Los Angeles
- Greater London
- Greater Rome
- Greater Paris
- Beijing
- Hong Kong
- Greater Tokyo
- Greater Delhi

COVENS

A coven is a group of vampires turned and controlled by a master vamp. When a master vamp turns a human, that new vampire has a deeper tie to their sire. This gives the sire/dam a modicum of control and power over the new vampire. Most masters who sire a new vamp will not put up with their new progeny refusing their control. Instead, the master will almost always choose violence, destroying the new vamp as a lesson to keep the rest of their coven in order.

Vlad tries to be scary, but he's usually pretty chill.
— G'snoort

THE COVENLESS

Those vamps turned by a non-master, and those whose master has been killed are considered covenless in vamp society. While they are much more independent, they also do not typically have the resources available to the coven-protected vamps. While the Conclave or the local Enclave may provide resources such as safe houses, food banks, or other material support for those under a coven, those resources are almost universally denied to the covenless.

THE BEAST WITHIN

Therianthropes have such a short lifespan compared to most of the Others, their society tends to be much looser in organization. There is no monolithic society like the vamps. Instead, groups of therianthropes are often arranged by the type of creature from which they pull their beast.

ORIGINS OF THE 'THROPES

For thousands of years, cultures from around the world have told tales of shapeshifters. Some, or most, of those legends have a grain of truth. True therianthropes, those who shapeshift from human to animal form, have somewhere, somehow been infected with some of the nightmare energy from *Coşmar*. There are tales of some of the Greek and other gods changing forms, but those are not the therianthropes of old. Either by curse, as in the loup-garou from the swamps of Louisiana, or by infection in their blood, like the werewolf or selkie, true therianthropes come in a wide variety of creatures that share their beast with their human host.

Therianthropes have been hunted throughout time as the hunters/killers that they are. Only by hiding in the night, and trying to blend into society can they survive. Whether their beast is a predator or prey animal, as creatures of the night and creatures of *Coşmar*, most therianthropes have an instinctive, intense hatred of vamps. And that hatred is reciprocated by the Conclave.

THE MODERN 'THROPE

The modern therianthrope is a human that generally tries to keep their beast in check, so they can live and work within human society for their shortened lifespan. With twenty years to live at most, a large percentage of therianthropes, especially the predators, become thrillseekers, trying to get the most out of their short life.

PACKS

Whether the beast within is a pack animal or solitary creature, either predator or prey, a lot of therianthropes form packs among their own kind. This becomes a mutual support group, often pooling living arrangements and resources. These packs are exclusively familial groups of the same therianthrope type, often being therianthropes from the same sires and dams.

Therianthropes are resistant to moving away from their pack, but if they are forced to move, due to a job or family, they search their new hometown area for a suitable pack that will accept them. The power and strength of the therianthrope is the determining factor in where the 'thrope stands in the pack, and who leads the pack as the alpha.

THE PACKLESS

When a therianthrope is without a pack, they often find it harder to maintain their human/beast balance. Without the resources and safety of the pack, finding a safe place to change and run on the full moon becomes very difficult. Oftentimes, the packless therianthrope becomes the target of a sanctioned hunt.

Packless can find help and resources if they can find a pack. Unfortunately, they often have difficulty putting themselves under a pack alpha if they have been on their own for a long time. Packless generally end up fighting for dominance in a new pack, and the outcome is never certain.

CHILD OF THE FAE

The children of the fae are those who share heritage with the fae and with humanity. Their dual heritage leads to strengths and weaknesses that neither of their heritages faces. Because they are the progeny of the fae, they maintain a somewhat muddied connection to the fae realm *Álfheimer*.

ÁLFHEIMER

The realm of the fae is a strange and ethereal realm. Few humans have ever experienced *Álfheimer*, and fewer still have returned from the realm. The *Álfheimer* is a wild, magical place where geometry does not quite work, and the creatures who inhabit the realm are filled and formed by the wild magicks.

FAE ON EARTH

Over the millennia, the fae creatures have come to the Earth realm and have interacted with humanity. From the Celtic legends and tales all the way to the modern era, the fae are present on earth. The fae are principal signatories of the *E'Tuatha Accords*, a treaty that keeps the fae and humans, and the other signatories, at peace. The Accords provide a way to keep the peace between the signatories while stating fully the obligations the signatories have toward each other.

THE COURTS

The fae are governed by the various Courts from *Álfheimer*. The Seelie Court is considered the light court and generally works to keep the peace among the Accord signatories. The Unseelie Court is considered the dark court and generally works to foment problems among the Courts and among the Accord signatories. Finally, the Seanachaidh is concerned with mediating between the Courts and between the fae and the Accord signatories.

SEELIE COURT

The Seelie Court is run by Her Majesty Lishe ta Merunaré, the Queen of the light elves (Lo'a). According to law and tradition, the Queen is technically married to the King of the Unseelie Court, although the two are diametrically opposed, and do not reside in the same castle. Tó Coferal, another Lo'a, is the Queen's Knight and her loyal companion.

Lo'a tend to be beautiful and even more ethereal than movies based on J. R. R. Tolkien's works showed them to be. The Queen is accompanied by her Maidens, a very deadly group of pixies trained in combat and dedicated to the protection of their Queen.

Tar Katel, a minotaur, is the head of the Queen's royal guard. Leading the Lo'a armies are Bearkinos Feralson and his mate Azriandra Darkshade, a pair of minotaurs that are renowned for their fighting prowess and leadership.

Some of the other races that make up the Seelie Court are the pixies and fairies, the minotaur, selkies, centaur, nymphs, satyrs, and gnomes.

Unseelie Court

The Unseelie Court is ruled by His Majesty King Arkanai t'Nakót, the King of the dark elves (Drauch). According to law and tradition, he is wed to the Queen of the Seelie. The Unseelie Court is ruled by the King's iron fist, and the King's commands are enforced by his Knight and Protector, Ugonan Ortá. The Drauch tend to have sharp features, dark, almost coal black skin, and black or gray hair–similar to a race of underground elves from a popular roleplaying game.

The Unseelie Court's warriors and armies are primarily made up of trolls and orcs. Merfolk, goblins, barghests, and boggarts are among other races that are typically found in the Unseelie Court.

Gray Court

The Gray Court is also called the Seanachaidh. They are the Keepers of the Law and the Peace. Their responsibility is to maintain the balance of the Courts, ensuring that the Courts follow the laws and traditions as written. The Seanachaidh is primarily comprised of dwarves and is divided into two governing bodies.

The Khozten are the Keepers of the Law. They are the scholars and jurists, arbitrating grievances and handing down pronouncements of guilt or innocence. Oracle Telacus Sturmwargh is the leader of the Khozten, and his Arbiter is Eraste Thrughar a female dwarf who is the Oracle's Hand of Justice.

The Khoztak are the Keepers of the Peace. They are the warriors and enforcers of the Courts, enforcing compliance and sanctions through any means, including threats of violence or actual violence. Praetorian Urteghat Dhorjachen is the leader of the Khoztak warriors. She leads the warriors with her prowess on the battlefield and her toughness off the field. The second-in-command Protector is a male dwarf named Dhaviha Chrechank, who is the Praetorian's Hammer of Peace.

Believe me, the Seelie Queen is so much nicer than the King. I should know. I used to be Unseelie.
    — G'Snoort

THE FAELING

As a child of both the fae and humanity, the faeling is caught between both worlds. They can often find a place among humanity, as long as their fae heritage is kept hidden as much as possible. Unfortunately for the faeling, they are considered less than fae by those from *Álfheimer*. Even though they retain some of their connection to the fae realm, any faeling that serves in the Courts is often relegated to the lowest status. Life can be difficult for the faeling, who often feel as if they have no home of their own.

PROGENY OF A PANTHEON

The pantheons are vast and varied. A pantheon is a collection of all the deities of a religion, like the Greek gods and goddesses. While each pantheon generally comes from its own realm, the deities of those realms can usually cross into the Earth realm with ease. The belief in those pantheons gives the deities their power in their own realm, as well as the Earth realm.

Some of the most common pantheons are:

- Greek
- Roman
- Norse
- Inuit
- Hindu
- Aztec
- Buddhist
- Hopi
- Egyptian
- Chinese
- Celtic
- Incan
- Navajo
- Sumerian
- Mayan
- Yoruba
- *Rhy'ctharn*
- The Mouse*

*The Mouse is an Earth-realm deity with primary temples in Anaheim, California, and Orlando, Florida.

DEITIES ON EARTH

The deities of the various pantheons occasionally show up on earth to interact with humanity. Most of the time, their appearance on earth is rather banal, unnoticed by the public or even their followers. At other times, those appearances turn into a dalliance with humans. Some of those dalliances with humans create the progeny called demigods.

THE DEMIGOD

As a child of both the gods and humanity, the demigod shares their heritage between two realms. While not fully human, they are also not immortal deities, and thus have no true home in their parent's pantheon, either. Demigods tend to have an easier time than faeling fitting in with humanity. Depending on the deity and pantheon involved, the deity may choose to be a part of the demigod's life.

Ah, Imp. He gets into, and out of, so much trouble. At some point, he's going to tick off the wrong diety...

— G'snoort

THE CRYPTIC CRYPTIDS

Bound to the natural Earth Realm, the cryptids are those unusual creatures that hide from humanity, making themselves legend and conspiracy. Although they are from the natural realm, the cryptids are wide and varied species and are found all over the world. Found on land, in the water, and even in the air, the rumors and sightings abound of these natural wonders.

POP A 'SQUATCH

One of the most recognized, and most elusive of the cryptids is the sasquatch – just don't call them "Bigfoot". Bigfoot was the nickname of one sasquatch who consistently tried to appear mysteriously in as many photos as he could. After their family found out, Bigfoot was disciplined and learned from his mistakes, which is why the appearances stopped for a time.

Sasquatch live in large, clan-like families in the forest. Often found in the Pacific Northwest, they are also found throughout North American forests, all the way down into the forests in Florida and the Southeast. Most of the sasquatch try to stay out of the public eye as much as possible, however, some of them try to integrate into the Post-Dragonfire era of society.

And then there's WD-42.
They are decent enough...
especially if you happen to
have catnip...

— G'snoort

Conspiracies Abound

It does not take a tin foil hat to know about the conspiracy of the reptilians running the media and government. Even with their preternatural ability to blend in, the reptilians can sometimes still be discovered in society. Whether it's a tech company mogul, a social media company owner stiff and unnatural before Congress, or members of congress and a President that present themselves as robotic and unnatural, the mask occasionally slips, hinting at the truth underneath.

The reptilians hide in plain sight in human society. It is not only some of the tech moguls, politicians, and Hollywood executives that are reptilian but the lizard-folk are found in many strata of society. With their rigid caste system, the reptilian elites and drones do not occupy the same strata of society. The elites occupy the upper strata positions, while the drones are relegated to the lower strata jobs. If a drone does end up working into an upper strata position, they will either be forced to give it up or, if they are found worthy, elevated to elite status.

Falling with Style

Of the cryptids with wings, the gargoyles are the most enigmatic, most prevalent, and least noticed. Gargoyles tend to live in family-like clans in larger towns and cities, usually in and around taller buildings and churches. Gargoyles tend to be pack defenders, and will viciously attack any who attack their building or its inhabitants.

While the winged creatures look like they are made of stone, their appearances are deceiving. They do not have the density of stone. Their wings and body are not made to fly like the birds, instead, their wings give them the functional ability to glide from heights, even catching thermals to ride them like a hang glider.

Gargoyles find it almost impossible to blend in with society, instead hiding in the shadows, looking down from the lofty heights upon the world below. Once a clan finds their home on a building, they tend to be very territorial, and do not leave that building unless forced out by the inhabitants or a wrecking crew. Modern multi-story office building managers have been known to make agreements with gargoyles to keep them on-site, while providing for the cryptids' needs as they can.

Science Most Dangerous

Human scientific breakthroughs are amazing and help enrich humanity. Most of the time. Unfortunately, there is a sizable group of scientists who have decided that they will experiment to see if they can achieve a breakthrough, without considering whether they should achieve the breakthrough with the works of their disturbed, creative, and inventive masterminds. These scientists create horrors straight out of science fiction and fantasy, experimenting on unwilling captives or even their own bodies.

Mostly Human

Straight out of science fiction, genetically-spliced horrors are experiments gone wrong for mad scientists. Whether they use insects or animals or even marine life, these evil geneticists work to combine human and creature DNA on whoever they can, whether the subject is a volunteer or a prisoner.

If the now-changed experiment subjects break free, they find it difficult to hide in society and blend in. Physically, their genetic modifications make them stand out in a crowd. These experiments are stuck with their often inhuman appearance, and struggle to find any way to live in or out of society. The life of a genetically-spliced experiment is difficult at best, and unbearable at its worst.

The Life of an Addict

Addiction to drugs is a terrible life. When the drugs are experimental, humanity-enhancing drugs that have so locked the addict into their life that their body relies on the drugs, the life of that addict is even worse. Oftentimes, the addict to the designer chemical compounds is the scientist themselves. The chemical formulations are tailored specifically to enhance some aspect of their humanity past normal limits, which help destroy the rest of the human body in terrible ways.

These chemical addicts often have a rough life. Even if their chemical formulation does not change their appearance, the physical and mental addiction to the substance means they are constantly in need of their specific formula. If the components of the formula are unique or unusual, the addict often has trouble finding and maintaining a supply of their addiction. This can lead to a bleak existence for the addict unless they can find the help they need to keep them supplied with their formula.

So You Accidentally (On Purpose) Joined a Cult

The final subjects of this briefing are those that are related to eldritch cults and the horrors they worship. Cults that worship the eldritch gods from *Rhy'ctharn* have been around for millennia. Those dark and twisted horrors desire nothing more than being invited to invade the Earth realm. Normally, cultists and cult leaders can gain some power from their horrific masters, but they remain human while doing so.

Finding Redemption

Sometimes a cultist gets so steeped in the power and blessing of the eldritch horrors that they can be connected to *Rhy'ctharn* and invite the eldritch horrors to fill them with their corrupting energy. Those corrupted cultists can often pass as humans among society until they unleash their eldritch power to advance the work of their gods.

Sometimes, those same corrupted cultists wish to leave the service of the eldritch gods. Unfortunately for them, the corruption is permanent, marking them as eldritch horrors. When those corrupted do break free from their cults, they are often pursued by their old cult members, and sometimes have to resort to using their eldritch powers to escape. Those corrupted who have escaped are known as Redeemed.

The Redeemed have a special place in society. They try to stay under the radar when it comes to their former cults while trying to actively thwart the work of those cults. The majority of the Redeemed eventually find an organization that they can join to use their abilities and powers to fight the cults more effectively. Agencies like the Office of Transhuman Affairs will generally welcome a Redeemed into their fold to aid them in the fight to protect humanity from the ancient eldritch horrors.

Thank you for sitting through this briefing. There is much more information in the archives, and you should have clearance for most of it. If you have any questions, ask your liaison. As for me, I gotta' get back to the War Wagon. I'm sure Boomer has questions about the latest upgrade.

"Oof. Those are gruesome. That used to be the dryad?" The young woman looked at the full-color prints of a bloody scene in her hands.

"Yeah. That's what's left of Wildewood." Special Agent Brianna Wilcox smiled, showing her fangs. "When we escorted her into the Queen's presence, I thought she was going to pass out. The Handmaidens were particularly upset."

Special Agent Grace Leonardi gave a small smile and nodded, "I believe it. A dryad harvesting pixies? I'm surprised she wasn't caught before now." Leonardi was the team's liaison officer at Sanctuary. She glanced at the rest of the report in the folder. "Everything else looks like it's in order." She looked up at the vampire agent. "Do you need anything else?"

Wilcox smiled, looking even more terrifying with the display of sharpened teeth. "A week off? I know the team would love some downtime."

The other woman smiled, "I'll see what I can do. Get some rest."

The two agents parted, Wilcox walking toward the apartment she and her husband shared on campus. Leonardi gripped the folder in her hands and headed toward the Archives. She would file this with the appropriate classification, and then go check with forecasting to see if she could arrange some downtime. She knew that Wilcox had already briefed Director Vanhof, which meant the case was closed.

As Leonardi approached the door to the Warehouse, her SSP buzzed. Pulling the secure phone from her jacket pocket, she looked at the screen.

"Dammit." She muttered under her breath as she put her phone away and looked at the folder in her hands. Knowing that she had to file the report before she made her way to the mission briefing.

It took two minutes to properly file the report in Archives, and Agent Leonardi was almost running as she left the Warehouse and headed to the briefing room mentioned in the message. Three minutes later, the young liaison slowed to a walk and calmed her breathing before she entered the door.

"Close the door, Grace, and seal the door, please. You are the last one for this briefing." The speaker was a tall, thin man dressed casually in a button-down shirt and jeans. Operations Director Jonas "Ghost" Vanhof was standing at the front of the room. He motioned her to an open seat.

"This intel mission is an offshoot of Operation Wildewood." Director Vanhof started without any preamble. His briefings were always short and direct. "Wildewood was a complete success, and I understand the dryad in question will no longer manufacture the drug." Jonas looked at Agent Leonardi, "Your team did well, Grace. Unfortunately, they won't be getting any rest. They have a new mission, and it is even more time sensitive."

The Director of Operations turned back to the rest of the room. "We're calling this one Operation Dragon's Blood. Apparently, Nora Wildewood's operation was not the only Dragon's Eye manufacturing facility. We just got word that there are at least two more, and the new variant is being cut with vampire blood. Forecasting is predicting a twenty percent chance that this will lead to a new vamp outbreak, and those odds are way too high for us to ignore."

A hand went up in the back of the room. "What's the target area, Boss?" Special Agent John "Spooky" Smith spoke up. "How big is the area?"

"Two areas, Spooky. Washington DC and Los Angeles." There were soft curses around the room. Ghost looked around the room, nodding. "That was pretty much my reaction. This one needs two teams."

The projector at the back of the room lit up, and the screen behind Ghost showed the team rosters. "Grace, you will gather The Wilcoxes and their team. I'm seconding Paladin to them as well. I've already talked with him, and he will meet them in LA."

Grace nodded, sending messages to her team. It was good news that they would have Paladin along, they could use the experienced agent. Pete "Paladin" McCarthy had been an independent agent before the program had even started, but had the experience of defending Sanctuary from the attack during Operation Dragonfire.

The Director went on, "Badger? You are going to join Bad Wolf and her team in DC."

The two people in the front row nodded and looked at each other. Special Agent Rob "The Badger" O'Neil was a solid man just under six feet tall. With glasses, graying hair, and a short, well-trimmed beard, the agent looked like an accountant or office drone. Until you noticed body armor across his chest and the large handgun strapped to his thigh.

The young woman next to him stood just over five feet tall, with long dark hair, hazel/green eyes, and a half-smile that spoke of mischief. Special Agent Amanda "Bad Wolf" Watkins was the team leader for Knightfall, a younger action team that currently was breaking in two new vampire agents.

Ghost looked back at the two tech specialists in the back of the room, "Spooky, you and Spooks build two teams. I want a tech team assigned to support each team. This operation is currently Classified as Red, but if the new variant starts turning people, we will escalate to Black. We've been assured of cooperation from the Seelie Court, and Dancer is working with the Gray Court to get their support as well. Go to it. Dismissed."

As the agents in the room stood, Spooky looked at the young woman next to him. "You want to put together the teams?"

Special Agent Christina "Spooks" Swanson was shorter than the red-headed tech. An amazing tech in her own right, Spooks and Spooky made an unstoppable combination. She nodded her assent, "Yeah. I'll get a list for you so you can submit it to Ghost." Her unmistakable Australian accent was undiminished by her years in the states.

The two tech specialists were the last ones exiting the briefing room. Thick as thieves, Spooky leaned closer to his partner in crime, "Usual bet? Last one to find the bad guys buys dinner?"

Spooks nodded and smiled. She had only bought dinner once.

SPECIAL AGENT MEMORIAL WALL

DRAGON'S EYE
- Brianna Wilcox - Page 9
- Michael Wilcox - Page 11

CHAPTER FIVE
- Bearkinos Feralson - Page 138
- Azriandra Darkshade - Page 138

AFTER ACTION REPORT
- Grace Leonardi - Page 146
- Pete "Paladin" McCarthy - Page 147
- Rob "The Badger" O'Neil - Page 147
- Amanda "Bad Wolf" Watkins - Page 147

Other Type:_____________________ Subtype:_______________

Age Stage:_________________________ Clan/Family:_____________

TALENT NAME

TALENT NAME

TALENT NAME

TALENT NAME

THE OTHER HANDBOOK

THE OTHER CHARACTER RECORD

THE OTHER HANDBOOK

THE OTHER BACKGROUND RECORD